SITTING DUCK

He took three steps and didn't hear the rifle shot that boomed across the street and shattered a storefront window just inches in front of his face. Longarm instinctively knew that the ambusher was going to fire again and dove through the nearest open doorway as a second bullet struck a pickle barrel and created a stream of sweet-smelling pickle juice that drenched the legs of his pants.

Drawing his gun and trying to scoot free of the stinking juice, he turned and surveyed the street, then the windows of every building where an ambusher could hide and take good aim.

Longarm jumped up and ran down an aisle out onto a small loading dock. He sailed off the dock into the alley, and in a few moments he was back on the main street.

From a second-story hotel room window just up the street, Longarm saw a curtain waving slightly in the breeze. Nothing unusual about that except that the next thing he saw was a rifle barrel sneaking out from under the curtain looking like a snake coming out of a hole . . .

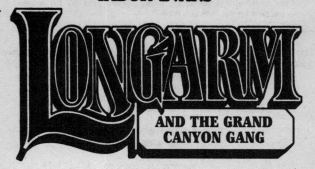

TABOR EVANS

LONGARM

AND THE GRAND CANYON GANG

JOVE BOOKS, NEW YORK

LONGARM AND THE GRAND CANYON GANG

A Jove Book / published by arrangement with
the author

PRINTING HISTORY
Jove edition / February 2004

Copyright © 2004 by Penguin Group (USA) Inc.

For information address: The Berkley Publishing Group,
a division of Penguin Group (USA) Inc.,
375 Hudson Street, New York, New York 10014.

ISBN: 0-515-13685-9

A JOVE BOOK®
Jove Books are published by The Berkley Publishing Group,
a division of Penguin Group (USA) Inc.,
375 Hudson Street, New York, New York 10014.
JOVE and the "J" design
are trademarks belonging to Penguin Group (USA) Inc.

PRINTED IN THE UNITED STATES OF AMERICA

10 9 8 7 6 5 4 3 2 1

Chapter 1

It was a fine Saturday morning in Denver when Deputy Marshal Custis Long rented a carriage from Delaney's Stables and watched Delaney hitch it up to a beautiful sorrel mare with a flaxen mane and tail.

Delaney was an old Irishman who always had a cheerful smile and a quick wit despite his excessive fondness for whiskey. But today, he was sober and happy to be renting out his best carriage to his favorite law officer.

"And so, Marshal, will you be takin' a lady for a drive this fine afternoon?"

"I will," Longarm told him. "But I won't tell you her name and where I intend to take her, you old gossip."

Delaney guffawed. "Why Marshal, what makes you think that I care where you go?"

"I know you."

"Ah, I suppose you do!" the Irishman agreed. "You know me for an honest and hardworking man who has a great appreciation for good whiskey and an eye for beautiful women . . . which you share. So is this one a special beauty?"

Despite his age, Delaney was still a feisty and energetic man with a smile that revealed he was missing most of his front teeth thanks to his love of a good saloon brawl every Saturday night.

Longarm liked the old man and had shared many a glass of whiskey and tall tale with Delaney. And while the Irishman usually became combative when in his cups, Delaney had a good and generous heart. He was an easy mark for every hard luck story and charity in town, which was probably the reason he was always on the verge of being dead broke.

"The woman I'm taking out today is a beauty," Longarm admitted.

"And you'll squire her up into the cool mountains and have a picnic beside the river. Then a little buckin' and shakin' on the blanket perhaps?" Delaney winked lewdly. "Ah, of course you will, Marshal Long! But don't let the lady get sunburned where the sun isn't supposed to shine on her lily white skin."

Longarm shook his head in wonder. "Delaney, you're nothing but an old lecher."

"That's true enough. And I have my eye on a widow woman of only sixty years. She's a fine lookin' gal with a wheelbarrow full of money! Maybe I'll pleasure her enough that she'll decide I'm the man she ought to marry."

Longarm thought that unlikely. "You'll never marry again because you're too ornery and independent."

"Oh, you think so?" Delaney spat a stream of brown tobacco juice into the dirt as he finished hitching the sorrel mare to the carriage. "Well, this woman has fire and wealth, and I'm not as stupid as you might think that I'd let such a lovely prize slip through my fingers. And while

2

we're on the subject, it might do *you* well to think of marriage."

"Not me," Longarm told the liveryman. "I'm plenty happy being a bachelor and living life on my own terms."

"You say that now," Delaney replied, wagging his finger at the marshal. "But when you're my age . . . if you should be so fortunate to live that long . . . you might well change your mind and seek the company of a comely and passionate wife."

"Well," Longarm told him with a wink. "I've got about forty years before I'm as ancient as you, so I'll not worry about such things yet. And what about this mare?"

"What about her?"

Longarm placed his hands on his hips. "She's a fine looking horse, but she seems excitable."

"Oh she is!" Delaney told him with an exaggerated smile. "She's only four and is plenty frisky—like the woman you'll enjoy this splendid day. But be kind and gentle to her, and she'll give you everything you want."

Longarm climbed into the carriage. "I hope that's true. I just don't need a runaway or an accident. The lady I am taking out today is not what you would call adventurous, and she would not appreciate a wild ride."

"Oh, but she might surprise you!" The old man cackled. "*You* give her a wild ride and see if I'm mistaken."

"Delaney, you're hopeless," Longarm said with a laugh. "Can you still even get it up?"

"Straight and tall as a flagpole!" Delaney cried, looking insulted for an instant but then recovering with a piece of advice. "Marshal, you must always remember the famous words of the saint of all good fishermen who said, 'It's not the size of your worm that gets swallowed by the fish that counts . . . it's how well it wiggles!' "

"Bosh! No saint ever said that."

3

"And who's to say for sure one didn't?" Delaney demanded a moment before he puffed out his chest, flexed his still-impressive biceps, and did a little jig in the barn dirt.

Longarm couldn't help but laugh as he drove away wondering if the old Irishman had already sampled the hair of the dog. The mare was excitable as they entered the street, but he felt sure that he could keep her under a tight rein and his control. Besides, she and the carriage were impressive, and he had worn his finest suit and was feeling pretty cocky. Beside him, there was a thick woolen blanket and, with a little luck, it might serve well for . . . as Delaney said, a little "buckin' and shakin'."

The woman Longarm was taking out for a drive into the mountains was Miss Elizabeth Weatherford, the daughter of the most prosperous doctor in Denver. Longarm had admired Elizabeth for quite some time, but, thinking her well out of his reach, he'd only coveted her from afar. But less than two weeks earlier, while he was walking to work, a mugger had accosted Miss Weatherford by grabbing her purse and shoving her to the sidewalk. Longarm had been close, and it had been a difficult choice whether to first help the lady to her feet or go after the thief. Because of his southern and chivalrous background, he had helped Miss Weatherford up, asked if she were injured, and when she replied she was not, he had turned and went racing off after the mugger.

Fortunately, the thief was rather on the heavy side and not in good condition. Longarm had tackled the man before he'd run a block and then had thrashed him soundly on the pavement before hauling him erect and escorting him back to Miss Weatherford.

4

"I know you. You're Eddie Reid, and you've been in jail for this kind of thing more than once."

"No sir. You must have mistaken me for someone else."

"The hell I do," Longarm growled. "Get down on your knees and beg the lady's forgiveness for your unspeakable action."

The thug, noticing the large crowd that had gathered, summoned up his pride and refused. Longarm leveled him with a crunching right cross to the jaw that caused a remarkable change in the thug's attitude.

"Miss," he said, voice trembling and eyes glazed from the power of Longarm's punch, "I'm a swine who don't deserve to live, much less be in your presence. Please forgive me for the terrible deed I done!"

To Longarm's amazement, Miss Weatherford had taken pity on the thief and insisted that he be released on the promise that he would never again snatch a purse or pick a pocket.

"He won't keep his promise," Longarm had told the auburn-haired beauty. "He's a lifetime criminal who will never stop his stealing."

"I think that to forgive is to be divine," Elizabeth had told him. "But that aside, I am truly in your debt."

Longarm had swept off his hat, introduced himself to the beauty, then immediately suggested they go out to dinner. The dinner had been perfect, her kiss as sweet as nectar, but she had reluctantly stopped him at that point and wished him good night.

"But today," he said to himself as he remembered how, with each kiss her passion had heightened, "I just might get lucky and get far more than a hug and a kiss."

• • •

5

She lived with her parents on a street named Greenleaf in the best part of Denver, and when Longarm turned up the wide circular driveway, it was immediately apparent that her father had more money than he'd make in three life-times as a federal marshal. The sorrel mare was still danc-ing and prancing as they approached the carriage house, and Longarm was feeling pretty proud of the impression he must be making. He doubted very much if the grounds-keeper or the liveryman who stopped to watch him com-ing up the drive would guess that he was a low-paid federal officer of the law.

"It must be nice to be rich," Longarm said to himself as he admired dozens of colorful roses that were in full bloom, "to have a gardener, a housekeeper, a liveryman, and to live in a beautiful place like this."

It crossed Longarm's mind that if he really was after wealth, it was not inconceivable that he might court and even wed Miss Weatherford, thus becoming a part of this opulent, high-society life. But he shook his head, knowing that he would never fit in and that he'd become jaded and soon be looking for the kind of excitement and danger he now enjoyed in his low-paid but never boring line of work.

Miss Weatherford appeared in the mansion's doorway holding their picnic basket. She was beautiful, and Long-arm felt his loins ache with desire. Today, he again thought, might at last be the day when he tasted *all* her succulence, when he finally got to wiggle his worm.

Longarm grinned at the prospect. He raised his arm to wave at Miss Weatherford, but at that very moment, her small white dog shot out of the front door and sailed across the veranda toward the carriage. The miserable dog was clearly pedigreed and it couldn't have weighed five pounds wet, but it got under the mare's hind feet and started nipping. The panicked sorrel bucked and took off running. Longarm hauled back on the lines, but the mare was terrified and the next thing he knew, they were ripping through the rose garden and the thin iron wheels of the carriage were mowing the beautiful flowers like a scythe through winter wheat.

"Whoa!" Longarm bellowed, almost standing up in the carriage and leaning back on the lines with all his strength. One of the reins snapped, and suddenly, everything began to spin through the roses. Longarm felt himself being launched upward in a shower of broken limbs and flowers, then he came down on what was left of the unforgiving roses. Big, nasty thorns punched through his pants, shirt, and coat, and he was dimly aware of the carriage flipping over and the sorrel dragging it on its side through another flower garden.

"Oh," he moaned, now knowing how it felt to be impaled in prickly pear cactus.

Longarm was twisted into angles but reluctant and perhaps incapable of movement. He still heard the ferocious little dog yapping.

"Beauford! Beauford!" Miss Weatherford screamed.

Longarm managed to raise himself up on one elbow. Who in the hell was Beauford?

The dog had gotten scratched by the roses, and its muzzle showed a splash of blood. It also must have gotten a thorn in its paw, because it was limping and whimpering most pitifully. Longarm watched as Miss Weatherford swooped the dog up in her arms and then stomped her foot before marching over to him and shouting, "Marshal Long, look what you've done to poor little Beauford and my daddy's lovely gardens, you stupid, incompetent oaf!"

He dragged himself off the thorns. "But it was your

dog that started all the trouble. You saw it with your own eyes!"

His logic escaped her, and Miss Weatherford cried, "You should not drive a carriage if you cannot *control* the stupid horse!"

"But. . . ."

"Do you have any idea how much my father prizes his roses? And look at the other garden. Ruined! Everything is ruined because of your ineptness!"

"I was doing just fine until your damned dog attacked my horse."

"Phooey! I thought you were a man of ability, but you're a complete incompetent and an imbecile to boot!"

Longarm's face turned crimson with rage, and he struggled to form a rebuttal to her insults and unfairness. However, by the time he had the words, Miss Weatherford was already stomping off to her father's mansion with little Beauford clutched to her lovely bosom. Longarm turned and saw that the liveryman was gone but the gardener was still in sight and appeared to be in a state of shock. Instead of helping Longarm to his feet and plucking the thorns from his body, the Weatherford's gardener covered his face and wept like a baby.

Longarm took stock of his ruined clothing and the blood, and the dozens of thorns embedded in his person and shouted at the top of his voice, "This might be the sorriest damned day of my life! What kind of people live here?"

The gardener shook his fists at Longarm and cursed him roundly.

Longarm decided right then that Delaney's once-elegant carriage was going to become a permanent ornament in what was left of the Weatherford estate's gardens. He limped over and collected the sorrel mare while reaching for his pistol. He placed the pistol in the sorrel's ear and cocked back the hammer of his gun.

"Naw," he said after a long deliberation. "It wasn't your fault, nor was it my fault. It was *Beauford's* fault, and I'll kill that dog if ever I get the chance!"

Torn and bleeding, he rode the sorrel back to Delaney's stable, and when the old Irishman saw his beautiful horse all cut with thorns protruding from her shiny coat, he almost had a fit.

"What on Earth did you do to her, man?"

"If I told you the truth, you wouldn't believe me."

"Try me!"

Longarm quickly recounted the story and ended by saying, "The carriage is ruined. I'll pay you its worth, but I'll have to do it in monthly payments."

"Where is this mansion?"

Longarm's eyes narrowed. "What do you have in mind?"

"First I'm going to find and strangle that dog, then I'll shoot the woman dead, and finally I'll try to salvage what I can of the carriage."

Longarm thought that sounded reasonable, so, still picking thorns out of his hide, he told Delaney where to find the Weatherford mansion and then promised to pay Delaney an extra fifty dollars if he also shot the gardener.

Chapter 2

Longarm was still angry the next day when he went into work at the federal building on Colfax Avenue. Given that his face was all scratched up, he got a lot of curious looks, but no one dared to ask him what tragedy had occurred.

No one except his boss, Billy Vail. "All right," Vail said, "everyone in this entire building is a'twitter about what happened to you this weekend. Some say you must have gotten hold of a real bad woman. Me, I think you tried to screw a bobcat."

Billy thought himself quite the joker, but Longarm didn't think it was a bit funny. "I'm in no mood for your bad humor," he said, plopping down in one of Billy's office chairs.

"Sorry, Custis," Billy replied, not sounding a bit sorry. "What did happen?"

"Roses." In a few terse words, Longarm explained what had happened at the Weatherford estate.

"My oh my!" Billy exclaimed, sitting down and kicking his feet up on his desk. "You really did screw up. Dr.

Weatherford is known far and wide for his rose garden and ornamental horticulture."

"I don't know about any 'horticulture,'" Longarm groused, "but he's got a new carriage ornament out in the front of his place. As for the horse and carriage, Delaney was sure steamed, and I owe him a couple month's worth of wages for wrecking his rig."

"Sounds like you had a hell of a bad day," Billy said.

"I did. But at least I learned that I don't ever want to get sweet on high-society women again. To tell you the truth, Miss Weatherford reminded me a lot of an overripe peach. They might still look great on the outside, but they're rotten on the inside. That woman gave me hell when the cause of the trouble was her own damned dog! Can you imagine?"

"Yes, I can," Billy said. "As a government employee, I've never hobnobbed with Denver's high society, because I know they think different than us common folks."

"They sure do."

"Is the rest of your person as torn up by thorns as your hands and face?"

Longarm frowned. "What's it to you?"

"Well, I was just thinking that . . . looking the way you do . . . it'll kind of put a crimp in your womanizing."

"I'm swearing off the opposite sex for a while."

"That'll be the day," Billy said. "Our new secretary, Miss Ordella Jensen, has been drooling over you since I hired her last month, or haven't you noticed?"

"I hadn't," Longarm said truthfully. "Which one is she?"

"She's got long brown hair and is in her late twenties."

"You mean the tall one with big breasts and hair piled on top of her head so it looks like an eagle's nest?"

"That's Ordella, all right. She's a good secretary, but

12

whenever you're around, she's so distracted that it's almost impossible to get any work out of her."

"Too bad," Longarm said, "because she's not my type."

"I'd say you don't have any type right now," Billy argued. "Not given the way you're looking."

"Never count me out," Longarm warned. "When I'm ready for the women again, I'll do fine. But let's talk business."

Billy nodded. "I was just coming to business. We have a problem in Arizona."

"That's not good," Longarm said. "Arizona is hotter than blazes in August."

"You're thinking of the desert part of the territory. But it's cool all year 'round in northern Arizona," Billy said. "And the trouble I'm talking about is up near the Grand Canyon in the Ponderosa pine country."

Longarm drew a cigar from his shirt, bit off the tip, and stuck it in his mouth without a light. "Last time I was anywhere near the Grand Canyon there was nothing except ranches and a few little railroad towns. As I recall, that was cattle and sheep country, and a big chunk of it was on the Navajo Reservation."

"And how long has it been since you were in northern Arizona?"

"Maybe six, seven years."

"It's changing fast, Custis. Flagstaff is a pretty good-size town. Lots of lumbering in addition to some huge ranches. Williams and Prescott are also growing, but I'm afraid there's a gang operating in that country."

"What about the local law?"

Billy leaned back in his office chair. "Flagstaff's town marshal was gunned down by the gang last month during a bank robbery."

"No replacement?" Longarm asked.

"Not so far. The town council has been warned not to hire a replacement or he'll also be shot."

"And they're caving in to that kind of threat?"

"Apparently. Or perhaps they just haven't been able to find anyone brave enough to pin on the badge. In the meantime, the gang is running wild."

"Doing what?"

"They're raising hell with the Santa Fe Railroad. They've hit the train three times and not only robbed the passengers, but also shot the engineer and two conductors. I've got a telegram from the Santa Fe saying their employees are so afraid of getting the same that they're refusing to operate on that stretch of high country and that there is a real danger that the railroad will have to cease operations."

Longarm chewed thoughtfully on his cigar and then said, "Billy, it sounds like a railroad problem to me."

"It is, but because the gang has absconded with U.S. mail, it's become a federal problem, and that means we have to deal with it."

"Yep, the theft of U.S. mail is a federal offense," Longarm agreed. "What do you know about this gang?"

"I'm afraid we don't know much. They wear masks, hit hard and fast, then disappear for as much as a week. They usually arrive on horseback, but twice they've boarded the train posing as passengers."

"How many are in the gang?"

Billy shook his head. "Could be as few as five or as many as ten. Sometimes, they strike simultaneously at different locations."

"Maybe there is more than one gang doing all the damage?"

"Maybe," Billy said, "but my hunch is that they're all in cahoots and they're not selective. By that, I mean they're suspected of stealing cattle from the local ranchers. They've also hit a couple stagecoaches, lumber mills, and mines."

"So they cover a lot of ground."

"You bet they do," Billy said. "Custis, I wish I could tell you more, but my information is scanty. All I've got are some desperate-sounding telegrams from Flagstaff, Williams, Prescott, and some little railroad town called Seligman. This gang is also suspected of having killed a rancher for his horses somewhere near the Grand Canyon, and even the Navajo Indians are complaining that several flocks of their sheep have been rustled."

Longarm's eyes widened with surprise. "You're not serious. Who ever heard of a gang of sheep rustlers?"

"This might be a first," Billy admitted. "All I know is that one of the telegrams says that the Navajo are pretty upset about it, and they're ready to take the law into their own hands and take scalps."

"Let them," Longarm said.

"That could cause even bigger problems," Billy warned. "The public is still jittery about the Indians, and the Navajo don't need any more troubles than we've already caused them."

Longarm lit his cigar. "Does this gang that seems to be everywhere at once and willing to steal anything of value have a name?"

"They're being called the Grand Canyon Gang."

"Serve them right if they did get scalped."

"Sure it would," Billy said, "but that wouldn't help get back the mail that was stolen or the money lost by the Navajo or all the other victims. And it wouldn't be a white man's justice."

"Scalping would be justice all the same," Longarm argued.

Billy dropped his feet on the floor. "Custis, we've got a tough job to do in northern Arizona, and we have to act fast before the Navajo and a lot of other people take matters into their own hands."

"Sounds like a job for *several* federal marshals."

"I can't spare but one, and you're my best man. Will you do it?"

Longarm grinned. "Have I ever turned you down, Billy?"

"No."

"That's right, and I'm not going to start now."

"Good! Custis, I know you just returned from a tough case in Montana two weeks ago and that this rosebush fiasco at the Weatherford estate sort of has you in the dumps, but you can rest on the train going out there."

"High country, huh?"

"Cool and green. Elevation about seven thousand feet. Sweet air and wide open spaces."

"I'd like to stay an extra week and see the Grand," Longarm told his boss. "I'm way overdue for a vacation. You're overworking me, Billy."

"That's because you're by far my best deputy marshal. I save the toughest jobs for you, Custis, which ought to be flattering."

"I'm tired, Billy."

"Then take two weeks of vacation in northern Arizona after you've dealt with the Grand Canyon Gang and everything has returned to normal."

"I can have *two* weeks?"

"Let's say ten days," Billy replied, hedging. "And I hear that Prescott is a great town for your kind of fun."

"And just what is my kind of fun, Billy?"

Billy winked. "Custis, your kind of fun is plenty of

good whiskey, music, and wild women. Can you leave this afternoon?"

"Afraid not," Longarm answered. "I'll catch the train tomorrow afternoon, but I want a generous expense account."

"How generous?"

"Generous enough so I don't have to return to Denver in the damned railroad cattle car like I did when I ran out of expense money in Montana."

Billy raised his eyebrows in mock outrage. "Be reasonable, Custis. It's not the government's fault you gambled away all your government travel money and spent the rest in a wasteful manner."

"Damnit, Billy, I was robbed!"

"By a floozy you took up with of your own free will." Billy looked pained. "Custis, we both know you're a hard man on criminals but far too naive and trusting when it comes to attractive but immoral women."

Longarm started to protest but then changed his mind, because Billy was right. He was too trusting of women, especially if they were young and beautiful. He just couldn't get used to the notion that beautiful women could be very treacherous and calculating. He'd even misjudged Miss Weatherford, thinking her refined and fair-minded when she'd proven herself to be just the opposite.

"When can I collect my Arizona travel money?"

"I'll meet you at the station tomorrow with the money and a round-trip ticket to Flagstaff."

Longarm climbed painfully out of his chair. "Billy, remember that you're sending me into rough country. I'm going to have to rent a good horse, saddle, and pack supplies if I expect to track down the Grand Canyon Gang. When I was sent to Montana, this office was so stingy that I had to rent an old sway-back plug that galloped like it was always traveling up a mountainside wearing hobbles."

"Aw, come on now!"

"I mean it. And the saddle I was forced to rent was as worthless as a four-card flush."

"No!"

"I'm serious," Longarm said, getting mad thinking about how poor an outfit he'd had to make do with in Montana. "I was chasin' one of the thieves on horseback when my cinch busted and I was almost beat to death under that old horse. It took me two weeks to recover and an extra month to catch my man."

"Custis, you always have to expect the unexpected."

"Yeah? Well, this time I expect a fair chunk of travel money. I'm going to eat right, sleep in a good bed when I can, and try to live like a successful human being instead of some poor jasper who doesn't have two plug nickels." Longarm bit down on his cigar. "I mean it, Billy. This time I go well heeled with government expense money or I'm staying in Denver and taking my vacation."

"Alright. Alright! You'll be traveling first class."

"Really?"

"That's right. And tomorrow at the train station I'll provide you with one hundred dollars in expense money."

"That's not enough given the tough assignment you've just outlined for me in northern Arizona."

"Custis, you can wire us asking for additional funds if they are legitimate and necessary."

"One-fifty cash in advance," Longarm said, folding his arms across his chest and jutting out his square jaw. "I'll bring back what I don't need and turn it in to our accounting department."

"Bosh! Custis, you'll spend every last cent, and we both know it."

"How much do you want the best man you got to go to Arizona?" Longarm demanded. "Enough to pay him so he can do his job without living like some poor beggar?"

"You win," Billy said, coming to his feet. "But if you foolishly allow some scheming young vixen to rob you of your travel money, I'll still expect you to bring the Grand Canyon Gang to justice."

"And I'll do it," Longarm promised as he started for the door.

"Don't you have some paperwork to do now?" Billy asked.

"Probably, but instead I'm going back to my room to soak in the bathtub. I still have a few rose thorns buried in my hide that I hope to soak out before I board a train tomorrow."

"I doubt a soaking will offer the slightest bit of help."

"Perhaps not, but it's worth a try," Longarm told his boss. "At the very least I'm going to catch up on my sleep until it's time to catch the train."

"I doubt that as well."

"That's because you really don't know me."

"I know you inside out, Custis. You're hell on wheels with the ladies, but right now you're one sorry sight and no attraction to any woman."

"Is that right?"

"Yes, it is."

"Bet me?"

Billy shook his head.

At the door, Longarm turned and said, "What did you say that new secretary's name is?"

His cheeks flushed with genuine anger. "Custis, leave my new secretary alone!"

"Ah, yes," Longarm sighed, snapping his thumb and middle finger, "Miss Ordella Jensen."

"Don't even look at her," Billy warned. "She's a very decent young lady, which means she wouldn't be interested in a two-timing rogue like you."

"Billy, I'm deeply wounded by your words," Longarm said, trying to look hurt and offended but not succeeding.

Had Billy already forgotten that he'd just agreed to go out on another tough assignment on very short notice? And besides, although he might look like hell with his face scratched up so bad, that didn't mean he still didn't yearn for some female company and one last night of red-hot lovin'.

Chapter 3

Longarm was halfway out of the federal building and had decided to forget about Miss Ordella Jensen when she rushed out of a first-floor office and almost collided with him.

"Excuse . . . my heavens! What happened to your face, Marshal?"

He smiled bravely. "I'm afraid it's a long and not very interesting story. Suffice it to say that I had a bad encounter with some rosebushes. They aren't looking so good, either."

"You really got scratched up," Ordella said, starting to reach up to touch his poor face and then changing her mind. "Does it hurt?"

"Not much. I've still got some thorns imbedded in my skin where I can't reach them."

"Well then, you should see a doctor and have them removed," Ordella told him. "Otherwise, they will fester."

"I expect they will," Longarm replied. "But I'm being sent to northern Arizona on the train tomorrow, and there just isn't time."

"But you just returned from Montana!"

"That's right."

"It's not fair that you should have to return to the field so quickly. I don't mean to sound critical of Mr. Vail, but you're being overworked."

"I told him the exact same thing." Longarm judged Ordella to be about five foot eight with brown eyes and a flawless complexion. Her nose was a bit too large and her mouth the same, but she was wearing some kind of perfume that quickened his senses and he could see that she was far more buxom than he'd initially thought. All in all, she was not a bad looking woman, although not beautiful in the sense that Elizabeth Weatherford was.

"Well," she said, frowning deeply and looking quite distressed, "I'm just a low-level secretary, but I'd be willing to speak to Mr. Vail about the unfairness of you being sent out so soon and in obvious pain."

"Thanks," Longarm said, "but I agreed to go and that's the way of it. Billy says there's a gang operating near the Grand Canyon, and he really needs me to go there and put a stop to their lawlessness."

Her brown eyes widened. "You're being sent to take care of an entire gang of outlaws?"

He shrugged his broad shoulders as if it were a small thing. "He said there probably aren't more than a dozen members of the Grand Canyon Gang."

"A dozen!"

"Yeah," Longarm said, "but generally speaking, all you have to do is catch and hang the ringleaders and then the followers either stop breaking the law or else disperse and cause no more trouble."

"I see."

Longarm smiled. "But I will admit that I have a few of those thorns in my hide that sure bother me."

"I should think so. Ah, where are they located?"

"Mostly on my back and some on my upper legs," Longarm said. "I don't suppose you'd be willing to help remove the worst of them, would you?"

Ordella smiled. "How could I refuse a brave federal marshal in need?"

"Could you come to my apartment?"

"Of course!"

Longarm gave her his address and best smile. "When can I expect you?"

"Would an hour be too soon?"

"You could get off work that quick?"

"I'll just say I'm feeling a little under the weather, and Mr. Vail won't mind. However, I could just tell him the real reason I want to leave early and . . ."

"I don't think that would be such a good idea," Longarm told her. "Billy and I are good friends, but he sort of frowns on his people socializing with each other."

"But this isn't a social call," Ordella said, batting her eyelashes. "This is an . . . an errand of mercy."

"Yeah," Longarm agreed, dipping his chin. "It sure is. See you in an hour."

She gulped hard and giggled. "It might not even be that long, Marshal."

"Custis," he corrected. "Custis Long."

"Ordella," she replied, blushing deeply as he turned and walked away.

Longarm returned to his apartment with a bottle of good whiskey and a box of chocolates for the lady. He quickly changed the dirty sheets on his bed, washed the dirty dishes in his sink, and generally tidied up his small, two-room apartment. He had to admit it wasn't a very attractive place to live. It was on the second floor of a brownstone building, and most of the tenants were either oldsters living on very little money or else young couples struggling to keep their heads afloat while building their families and careers.

But the rent was right and the couple just below him watched all visitors, so Longarm felt he could go away for weeks and never had to worry about a break-in. Furthermore, there were two young women who roomed together just down the hallway, and he had a hunch that he would one day get to know them on a very intimate basis. The trouble was, he was so often on assignment that there just hadn't been either the time or opportunity to get to know the girls better.

He was taking out the trash when Ordella appeared in the downstairs lobby. "Well, hello! You're here early."

"I couldn't bear the thought of you being in pain, so I left almost immediately after you did. Mr. Vail wasn't at all upset. I think he approves of me."

"I think so, too," Longarm said, not adding that she had been the subject of controversy between himself and Billy Vail. "I'll empty this trash in the alley and be right back."

"I'll go with you."

"All right," he said, "but it isn't pretty back there."

"I'm not going to be shocked," she told him.

Longarm shrugged and carried his trash around the corner of the brownstone into the alley. He knew it was not a safe place to go, as there were derelicts and drunks who often used the alley as a place to sleep off their hangovers or just hide from the local law until it was dark, when they ventured out to steal whatever they could find to resell for liquor.

And sure enough, when they entered the dim alley, there were three men squatting on their haunches drinking rot-gut whiskey from a bottle. "Ordella," Longarm said in a low voice, "go on back and I'll be with you in just a minute."

Ordella sized up the situation and realized that she ought to do as he suggested. "Why don't we forget the trash and both go back?"

Longarm saw all three of the derelicts come to their feet and start toward him with expressions that did not fill him with brotherly love. He'd removed his side arm and badge when he'd started tidying up his apartment, so he was unarmed as well as outnumbered.

"Good idea," he said, backing up while keeping himself between the three men and Ordella.

"Hold it, mister!" the largest of the three commanded. "We're not wanting trouble."

"Then back off," Longarm warned. "I'm a United States deputy marshal, and I won't tolerate any trouble from you men."

"You're a marshal, huh?"

"That's right."

"Then where are your gun and your badge, Marshal?"

"In my apartment."

The big man chuckled meanly. "I don't believe a word of it. Say, who's the pretty woman? You come back here to do a little bumpin' and humpin', maybe?"

Longarm felt his anger coming to the boiling point. "I'm warning you, mister. All three of you go back to your whiskey and don't be causing me or this lady any trouble. Otherwise, I'll have to arrest you."

"Hear that Jake?" one said to their leader. "He's going to arrest the three of us even though he ain't got no badge, no gun, and no stomach for a fight."

"I heard him," Jake said, switching his grip on the nearly empty bottle of whiskey and then hissing. "Mister, we'll let you go, but we need some money. You got money, don't you?"

"No," Longarm told the thug. "My pockets are empty. I was cleaning my apartment. I do have some trash in this can you can have."

"Money is what we need. And that woman wouldn't hurt us, either. Would you, honey?"

Longarm had heard enough to know that he had only two choices, and they were to run . . . or to fight. And because he wasn't accustomed to running from trouble and didn't care to cultivate the habit, he decided to fight. But first, he had to get Ordella out of the alley just in case he were badly hurt or even killed.

"Ordella," he said, "you need to get out of here right now!"

"We *both* do, Custis!"

Before he could reply, the big man called Jake charged with his upraised bottle. Had Longarm been armed, he would have shot the man dead before he'd closed the distance, but now all Longarm could do was push Ordella back and brace himself for the charge.

Jake slashed downward, and Longarm dodged to the side then struck the large man with a wicked and perfectly timed uppercut that caught Jake at the hinge of his jaw. Everyone in the alley heard the heavy crack of bone followed by Jake's scream as Longarm kicked the big man in the belly as he was falling.

But the other pair was on him like a swarm before Longarm could straighten, and one of them had a knife. Longarm felt the blade slice across his ribs, probing for entry to his vital organs but glancing off bone. Longarm grunted and threw out a wild blow that knocked the man and his knife aside. The third man kicked Longarm in the side of his leg, just missing his knee. Longarm grunted with pain but grabbed the man around the neck and drove his head into the grimy brick wall again and again until the man went limp.

Longarm whirled to see the one with the knife coming at him again. Not willing to be stabbed a second time, Longarm scooped up an empty bottle and hurled it as hard as he could straight into the knife holder's face. The bottle shattered, and the man was blinded in an instant by shards of glass. Screaming, he turned and tried to run, but Longarm caught him in two strides and slammed him into the trash barrels and then knocked him senseless with his fists.

The fight was over. Ordella stood in the dim light that lanced down between the buildings and then reached for Longarm, whispering, "Did you kill them?"

"I doubt it."

"But you hurt them very badly."

"Yes," Longarm told her. "I did."

"Let's get out of here!"

Longarm surveyed the carnage. His heart was pounding, and he could feel blood warm and wet on his side. If Ordella hadn't been hugging him, he might even have gone back and exacted more physical damage . . . he was that angry.

"If I ever see any of you in this alley again . . . or anyplace else in Denver . . . I'll make you wish you were never born!" he shouted, turning away and allowing himself to be led back to his apartment.

"You've been cut!" Ordella said as she slammed the door closed and began to help Longarm out of his shirt. "Oh my goodness, you're bleeding!"

"Ordella, calm down," he said, still panting from his frenzied exertions. "It's just a little flesh wound. I've been stabbed deep before, and I can tell this isn't anything serious."

She finished removing his shirt and then studied the knife wound. "You're right," she told him after a few moments. "Does this hurt?"

"Ouch!"

"I guess it did. Have you got any bandages?"

"Yeah," he said. "In my dresser drawer there are some clean undershirts. We can tear one up and use that."

"Then we have to get you to a doctor."

"No, we don't," he said. "There's an unopened bottle of whiskey on the kitchen counter. Open it up and use it to disinfect the wound. Then get me a glass, and I'll medicate my whole body. The knife wound doesn't hurt any worse than those damned rosebush thorns."

"Oh, Custis, you're a disaster! How in the world do you expect to be on a train bound for Arizona given your condition?"

"I'll be on the train," he vowed.

"I brought some tweezers and a little bottle of iodine."

"Good," Longarm told her as he kicked off his boots and then his pants. "But first the whiskey."

"I'm going to need some, too."

"There's plenty for us both," he told her as he headed into the bedroom. "Let's get started."

Ordella turned out to be a very competent nurse and rose thorn-puller. While they sipped whiskey, she went over every square inch of Longarm's poor body, and it took her nearly an hour to remove each and every thorn.

"You've sure got a lot of scars," she told him when she'd finished bandaging his side. "I never saw a man with so many scars."

"I've been in a lot of bad scrapes," he admitted, looking up a her. "I'll bet a woman like you hasn't a single scar on her whole body."

28

"You'd lose that bet," Ordella said. "I got *two* scars."

"Where are they?"

"One's on my bottom. I was only a little girl when I was shoved down and sat on a sharp piece of tin. It cut my bottom real deep, and the doctor had to use six stitches to get it to stop bleeding. But of course, I can't see the scar."

"But I could."

She smiled. "And I suppose you'd like to see it, huh, Custis?"

"I would. But where is the other scar?"

"It's . . . it's on the inside of my thigh."

"Oh? And how did you get that?"

Ordella blushed. "I would rather not tell you, because how I got it is embarrassing."

Longarm was feeling the whiskey warm in his belly, and the pain of the knife and rose thorns was only a memory as he reached for Ordella and began to help her undress. "I don't mind if you don't tell me how you got the second scar," he told her as he kissed her cantaloupe-size breasts, causing her to nearly swoon. "Fact is, it's better that you don't."

"Really?" she breathed as he removed the last of her undergarments then rolled her over on her belly to examine the scar on her pretty bottom.

"Yeah, really," he said, kissing the scar. "Because I think it's good for a woman to have a little mystery about herself."

"Oh, that's nice," Ordella said as Longarm spread her legs and then slipped his finger into her honey pot.

She moaned and bit his pillow a moment later when he entered her from behind and began to slowly work them both into a frenzy.

"Oh, Custis," she panted as he moved a little faster.

29

"I've been dreaming about you and me doing it together. But I didn't think it would start with me lying on my stomach."

"You want me to turn you over right now?" he asked, his long tool deeply embedded into her hot wetness.

"Not yet," she groaned. "Just don't stop what you're doing!"

Longarm had no intention of stopping. When he took Ordella the second time, he would roll her over and take a quick peek at her second thigh scar but let her keep her embarrassing little mystery.

Chapter 4

"Well," Custis said to Ordella as the Denver and Rio Grande's huge steam powered locomotive blasted its whistle one last time and then jerked forward, headed down the southern track, "I'd better board this train, or it's leaving me behind."

"One last kiss!"

Longarm pulled the woman into his strong arms and kissed her with passion. "I expect to be back in a month. Six weeks at the longest."

"I'll be waiting," Ordella promised as Longarm swung up on the train and handed the anxious conductor his first-class ticket.

"You're cutting it mighty fine today, Marshal," the conductor said with a grin. "It seems you leave a new woman each time we have the pleasure of your company."

"Well," Custis said, waving at Ordella as the train rolled out of the train depot and gathered speed, "I like to keep my life interesting."

The conductor was a man in his mid-fifties with gray hair and a mustache. "So do I, but one woman is all I could ever stand at one time. Do you think you'll ever find that *one* woman, Marshal Long?"

"Probably not."

"That's what I figured. Well, there's nothing wrong with playing the field, I guess. It just seems like it would wear a man down after too many years."

"I don't worry much about that," Longarm told the conductor. "In my line of work, you sort of make hay while the sun still shines. Understand?"

The conductor laughed. "I sure do! Well, Marshal, we have a berth for you all the way down to Santa Fe. We're having good weather, so I expect your trip will be most enjoyable. I've only one question."

"What's that?"

"How did you wangle a first-class ticket for this trip from the bureaucrats? Usually, you go second class."

"I was overdue for a lengthy vacation," Longarm explained. "I've been working way too many cases, and I just demanded to go on this one first class. I also got a one hundred-dollar advance."

"My goodness," the conductor exclaimed, obviously impressed. "That's a lot of money."

"I might be gone for a month or more, and I'll have big expenses." Longarm smiled. "When you're after criminals, you can't ride bad horses, sleep in bad hotels, eat bad food, and live like a pauper. If you do, it catches up with you in a hurry. You wear down and risk making a fatal mistake."

"I understand," the conductor said, nodding his head in vigorous agreement. "Who are you going after this time?"

"They're being called the Grand Canyon Gang."

"Oh, I've heard of that bunch! They rob anyone and everyone, including the Navajo Indians."

"That's the ones, all right," Longarm said. "So I'm go-

32

ing all the way to northern Arizona on this trip."

"You'll be hooking up with the Santa Fe Railroad for most of your journey to the West."

"Yep," Longarm said. "And I'll be riding first class with them as well."

"Good for you," the conductor said. "I'll take you to your sleeping compartment. We've got one of the nicer ones reserved for you."

"Thanks," Longarm told the man. "Lead the way. The first thing I'm going to do is sleep all the way down to the New Mexico border."

"Yeah, you look like you could use some shut-eye. Say, what in the world happened to your face?"

Longarm didn't feel like explaining about the rose garden, so he said, "That was a wild woman I just left behind at the train station."

The conductor's jaw dropped. "Why, I've heard about wild women tearing up a man's back a mite in the midst of passionate lovemaking, but I never heard of one who scratched up his face."

"There are all kinds," Longarm said sagely. "I'd rather the one I just left had raked my back rather than my face, but things got out of hand, if you know what I mean."

The conductor shook his head and rubbed his jaw in amazement. "I don't reckon I do, but I have a good imagination. That woman didn't look *that* wild."

"Oh, but she was," Longarm said, gently turning the conductor around and giving the man a push toward the first-class coach.

Longarm felt important and like a winner as he nodded at the other first-class passengers and pretended that he'd bought the ticket on his own dime. Then, Longarm went into his private berth, reset the seats into a bed, and stretched out. The bed was a little short for a man of his height, but Longarm wasn't complaining. Ordinarily, he'd be scrunched up on a hard leather seat and trying to bend his neck to the side and get a few uncomfortable hours of sleep while sitting erect. But not this trip. Longarm pulled the shades over his little window to the world, puffed up his pillow, closed his eyes, and prepared for sleep, thinking of the last bout of lovemaking he'd had with Ordella and how much he was looking forward to returning to her passionate embrace.

No doubt his boss, Billy Vail, would somehow learn that his new secretary had been Longarm's latest conquest. And no doubt, Billy would be furious. But he'd get over it, and his anger would turn to envy, just as it always had whenever he'd learned that Longarm had bedded another of his government employees. Longarm just hoped that Ordella did not suffer from inevitable office gossip. People who were envious could be cruel, and Ordella didn't deserve that kind of treatment.

No, Miss Ordella Jensen was *real* special.

Longarm yawned, touched his scabby face, and hoped he would be looking normal by the time he got to Arizona. He liked the rocking of the coach and the clickity-clack of the iron wheels on the iron rails. In no time at all, he was sound asleep and began having an erotic dream of riding a joyous Ordella.

Longarm didn't awaken until dusk, when his train stopped for water and fuel at Raton Pass. He had slept all day and awoke feeling rested and hungry. He found a pitcher of fresh water and a fine porcelain wash bowl, which he used to refresh himself. When he gently patted his face dry, some of the scabs came off on the damp towel, and he nodded with satisfaction. He would be soon presentable and back to his normal appearance.

Longarm combed his damp hair, brushed back his fine handlebar mustache, and found his hat. After a couple excellent glasses of whiskey, he intended to have a splendid meal in the dining car. Who knows, he thought, perhaps there would even be a lovely and unattached woman there who he could meet. Not likely, of course, but Longarm considered himself an optimist.

When he arrived at the dining car, he was greeted warmly and escorted to a small table with fresh white linen and flowers.

"Will you have a libation before supper?" the dining room attendant asked.

"Yes, of course. Whiskey—your finest."

"Very good, sir!"

Longarm was seated so he could watch the other first-class passengers arrive in the dining car, and he noted that most of them were older folks. All were better dressed than himself and had huge gold chains attached to their pocket watches. They wore stiff collars and white shirts, and some even with buttons in their lapels. And while he nodded and smiled in greeting to these people, many chose to look down on him even though he was a fellow first-class passenger.

To hell with them, Longarm thought.

But then, as if his prayers were heard on high, a single woman with beautiful red hair and green eyes appeared in the doorway of the dining car. She wore a stunning dress, and every eye in the room was captured by her loveliness. Longarm's breath was taken away as the woman was escorted to a table next to his own.

"Thank you," she said in a slightly husky voice.

"Will the lady be eating alone tonight?" the attendant asked.

"Yes."

"Very good," he said. "Anything to drink?"

Her eyes touched on Longarm, and they were not judgmental or condescending. She looked back to the attendant and said, "I believe I'll have whiskey. Your finest, of course."

"Of course, madam!"

Longarm knew he was not looking his shiniest, but this opportunity seemed too good to ignore, so he gave the woman his best smile and said, "My name is Custis Long, and your beauty makes the flowers on my table seem drab by comparison."

Her green eyes widened a little, and she smiled. "I suspect you are a gentleman from the deep South, sir. Am I mistaken in that judgment?"

"No, you are not. I was born and raised in West Virginia. But I have never gone back since the war. Too many things have changed there, and not for the better, or so I am told."

"You were told correctly," she said. "The South was destroyed by Sherman's army, and it is slow to recover. Old wounds of such a terrible war will never heal, and I think it will take generations before the South will really sing again with any joy in her heart."

"Well put, Miss . . ."

"Alexander. Emerald Alexander."

"I never met a woman named Emerald," he said. "But it's clear that your name matches your eyes. Will you be going far?"

"Quite far. And you, sir?"

"To the Arizona Territory."

"How interesting."

36

Longarm raised his eyebrows in question. "And why, Miss Alexander, is that?"

"It just is," she said vaguely as her whiskey arrived.

Longarm loved a woman who had secrets. It offered such a challenge. "May I make a toast, Miss Alexander?"

"Of course."

"To our trips," he said. "And, most important, to the pleasure of the journey itself."

His toast must have amused her, because she smiled and raised her glass. They drank and then she said, "I have a rather personal question to ask, but I don't wish to insult."

"I'm sure you could not do that even if you tried."

"Not so," she countered. "I actually have quite a sharp tongue when provoked, but I wish you no embarrassment. However . . ."

"My face," he said, seeing her discomfort. "You are curious what happened to my face."

"Yes, I am! You're a very handsome man, but . . ."

He touched his cheek. "These are just thorn scratches. I . . . I had an unfortunate encounter with a rosebush."

Now she laughed, and he learned that she had a deep, throaty laugh that was quite engaging. "Sir, would you mind explaining how you found yourself in such a predicament?"

"It's a long story," he replied. "Would you mind if I join you so I don't have to shout over the sound of the wheels on tracks?"

Emerald studied his face and then made her decision. "Very well."

Longarm was seated at her table in the blink of an eye. It gave him no small measure of satisfaction to see the looks of disapproval from the stuffiest of the older folks who had earlier given him a snub. And he was quite sure that some of the older men were filled with jealousy, for their own wives were . . . well, uniformly unattractive and fat with double chins.

Longarm's only dilemma at the moment was if he should confess that he was just a low-paid federal deputy marshal. After all, this woman was obviously of the wealthier class, and she would probably find him much less appealing if he were honest about his profession and lack of finances.

"So what do you do, sir?"

"Custis," he said. "Custis Long at your service." He reached across the table and they shook hands. Her hand was large and her grip strong. He liked that and judged her to be about five foot five inches tall and about thirty years old. She was obviously no child and very much a woman of refinement and breeding. Why, the diamonds on her fingers were so large and stunning that he imagined they must have cost a small fortune.

"Well, Custis," she said, "what takes you to the Arizona Territory?"

"Banking," he blurted. "I have an interest in banking. And also ranching and the mail."

"The mail?"

Longarm realized that he'd misspoken, and he rattled his brain for an explanation. "I . . . I have worked for the federal government with the mail."

"Oh," she said, as if understanding. "You are a contractor who helps deliver the mail."

"Yes, sort of," he replied, knowing the hole he was already digging himself into. "I am actually more of a detective than a contractor."

"A detective?"

"What takes you to wherever you are going?" he asked, trying to artfully change the subject.

"I'm going to Santa Fe on family business."

"How nice." He wondered what kind of family business she was going to conduct but was too polite to ask.

"And then I am also going to the Arizona Territory."

Longarm beamed. "How nice! I'm going to Flagstaff."

"And I," Emerald said, "am bound for Prescott. It's the territorial capital of Arizona, and my father is in politics . . . among other things."

"No husband?"

She sipped her whiskey and studied his face. "Tell me the story of you and the rosebush."

"Bushes," he corrected. "In fact, a whole garden full of them."

"How interesting! I can't wait to hear the rest."

So Longarm told her about what happened with the fine carriage and the stupid horse and the little dog that created the fiasco. He told her the truth, leaving out nothing, and when he had finished, Emerald was almost in tears with laughter.

"Dear Custis Long," she said, finishing her whiskey. "I believe that is one of the funniest stories I have ever heard. You poor man!"

"I did not come off well that day," he said, wishing she would not laugh quite so uproariously. "I was the complete fool."

"Nonsense! It was the young lady who was the fool for letting her little dog destroy her father's rose garden. You were only an innocent participant in the whole unfortunate debacle."

While Longarm was trying to form a reply, the attendant reappeared and asked if they were ready to order supper.

"I'm not yet hungry," Emerald told him. "I think I'd like another whiskey."

"Me, too," Longarm said.

"Very good!"

As darkness fell and the train headed down to Santa Fe, Longarm completely lost track of time. He and Miss Emerald Alexander had a wonderful dinner and shared a bottle of very expensive French wine. And finally, when the lady's eyelids grew heavy, she said she was ready for her share of the check and sleep.

"Let me pay for it," he offered, knowing the tab would be steep but sure that he would be amply repaid with the pleasure of this woman's company either tonight or in the near future.

"No," she said, reaching for her purse. "That would not be fair."

"Of course it would!" he insisted, "as long as you promise that we can do this tomorrow night on the Santa Fe."

"Very well," she told him. "Knowing that you are a Southern gentleman, I can see that further insistence to pay on my part would only cause you discomfort. And thank you very much, Mr. Long."

"My pleasure!" He leaned forward so the few remaining diners would not overhear his next intimate request. "And may I escort you to your berth, Emerald?"

"I think not," she said in such a winning way that he did not feel completely disappointed. "But I very much look forward to your company in the morning."

"And the feeling is mutual," he gallantly assured the lovely lady.

"Good night!"

He smiled. "Good night."

When she was gone, Longarm reached into his pocket for his wallet but, to his shock and surprise . . . it was missing!

The attendant watched him fumble through all the pockets of his coat, then his pants but find no wallet. Longarm smiled and tried to sound nonchalant. "I must have misplaced it."

"Of course."

Longarm stood up, aware that everyone was watching him. "Could you just put this on my tab?"

The attendant's smile slipped. "This is not a saloon, sir. I'm afraid you need to pay for your meals now."

"Sure, sure," he said, at last coming to the realization that his wallet, his Santa Fe train ticket, and the hundred dollars of government travel money were not on his person. "I must have left my wallet in my sleeping compartment."

"Let's go see," the attendant said, his personality undergoing a change that was not for the better.

"Yes, let's do!"

Longarm was acutely aware of the snickers and suspicious looks he received as he departed the dining car with the attendant hot on his heels. When he arrived at his compartment, his heart was pounding and his supper had turned sour in his stomach. Yet one had to keep up a good face, so he stepped into his compartment, closed the little curtain behind him, then frantically went through his luggage and belongings until the cold reality of the thing hit him full in the face.

He had either lost his wallet or . . . or he'd been robbed!

Longarm took a deep breath and composed himself. He stepped out of his sleeping compartment and said to the attendant in an angry and offended tone of voice, "I've been robbed, and I demand to speak to the conductor!"

The man was half a foot shorter than Longarm and smart enough to do as he was told without offering insult to injury. "I'll go find him, sir."

"Yes, do that immediately!"

Longarm ducked back into his compartment and once again tore his luggage apart and then looked in every crack and cranny of the small compartment but did not find his wallet or money. Fortunately, his Colt revolver was still in his bag, as was his marshal's badge. And he had never been so foolish as to go completely unarmed, so his solid brass, twin-barreled derringer was still attached to the fob and his fine gold Ingersol Railroad watch.

How could he have lost his money? Or more likely, who could have gotten close enough to rob him?

Two names came immediately to mind. The only two people who had gotten near enough to him were . . . oh, impossible!

But yet, as he stood in his compartment waiting for the conductor and wondering how he would pay his bills on this trip, the only possible suspects who came to mind were Miss Ordella Jensen or Miss Emerald Alexander.

But Emerald was the daughter of a wealthy Arizona politician, while Ordella, well, who knows what her background might be?

Yes, Longarm thought, *it* had *to be that damned Ordella* and, concerning the retrieval of his travel money, that meant he was shit out of luck.

Chapter 5

When the conductor arrived, Longarm drew the man inside his compartment and said, "I've been robbed of all my money and the train ticket I had for the Santa Fe Railroad."

"How much money?"

"A hundred dollars. And my first-class ticket from Santa Fe to Flagstaff."

"That is a big problem," the conductor said. "I understand that you and Miss Alexander chalked up quite a hefty bill in our dining car."

"That's right. And I offered to pay it!"

"Someone has to pay it."

Longarm groaned. "I sure hate to ask Emerald to do that. It'll make me look like an idiot."

"I'm afraid it might," the conductor said. "But nevertheless, because you are entirely without funds, I have no choice but to ask her to pay for your evening. The bill is too large for me to ignore."

"Couldn't you just loan me some money against the dining room tab?"

"Sorry. Conductors don't make that much money, and it would set a bad precedent."

"Then what am I supposed to do between now and Santa Fe?"

The conductor shrugged. "I suppose I could bring you a little leftover food so you didn't get too hungry. Some bread and an uneaten salad, perhaps."

Longarm sagged on his bed. "I can't believe I've been robbed."

"Any idea who might be the guilty party?" the conductor asked. "Surely you didn't leave your wallet in this unattended sleeping compartment."

"No, I did not. Whoever took the money managed to get their hand inside my coat pocket. They had to be very, very skilled."

The conductor shook his head. "What about the young woman at the Denver train depot?"

"Yes," Longarm said. "She's the most likely culprit. But I am sure that Miss Jensen loves me and wouldn't do such a thing."

"Of course she wouldn't!" the conductor said, rolling his eyes and looking totally unconvinced.

Longarm asked, "What do you know about Miss Emerald Alexander?"

"Absolutely nothing."

"Has she ridden this train before?"

"Never."

Longarm frowned. "She told me she had business in Santa Fe and that she was going on to Prescott, Arizona, where her father was in politics."

"So?"

"So I wonder if that's true." Longarm scowled. "I mean, there is the slimmest of chances that she could be the one who lifted my wallet."

"Were you that close?"

Longarm thought hard. "Once, she excused herself for a moment, and when she returned I stood up and the train seemed to lurch a bit. Anyway, I caught her in my arms, and it was very nice."

"I'm sure it was, Marshal. But it might also have been very *expensive*. Perhaps you also bumped up against someone in the aisle while either coming or going from this sleeping compartment to the dining car."

But Longarm shook his head. "I don't think so."

"Well then," the conductor said, "that only leaves two real suspects, and both of them are attractive women. One is on this coach, and the other is still in Denver."

"Yes," Longarm said. "And I'm dead broke."

"Can you wire your superiors from Santa Fe requesting replacement funds?" the conductor asked.

"I could, but they'd be refused, and I'd be made to look like a total idiot." Longarm scowled. "I can't do that. There *must* be a better way."

"You're a United States Marshal, so that leaves out theft, doesn't it?"

"Yes. But I am a decent poker player. And if you would just lend me twenty dollars, I might get lucky and . . ."

"I'm sorry, Marshal Long." The conductor actually did manage to look sorry as he backed out of Longarm's sleeping compartment. "But now I must go and ask Miss Alexander if she will pay *your* bill."

Longarm swore under his breath. "That will be the end of our budding friendship."

"If so," the conductor told him, "I have no doubt that you will soon be able to meet another young woman, and that, somehow, by hook or by crook, you will find a way to recover your loss and get all the way to Flagstaff."

"A hundred dollars is a lot of money to recoup."

"For me," the conductor said, "that's three months' wages. Good luck and good night, Marshal Long."

Custis collapsed on his bed in a state of complete despair. How humiliating that Emerald was being asked to pay for their elegant dinner and drinks! So much for his so-called Southern chivalry! He desperately wanted to follow the conductor to Miss Alexander's compartment and insist that he be allowed some time to recover his losses and pay that dinner tab.

Instead, Longarm kicked off his boots, loosened his tie, and tried to go back to sleep. It wasn't easy, and he probably traveled twenty or thirty miles before that quest was accomplished. When he awoke, they were in old Santa Fe, New Mexico.

"Marshal Long?" the conductor said as Custis prepared to disembark at the train station.

"Yes?"

"Miss Alexander was gracious enough to assume responsibility for your supper bill."

"I'm very glad to hear that."

"Yes, she understood completely. Even told me that she had once had her purse stolen and found herself in an equally distasteful predicament."

"How much was the bill? I want to repay the woman, if she'll give me a chance."

"Eight dollars plus she gave us a dollar tip."

"That much!"

"Yes. Remember, you dined rather lavishly, and that whiskey you drank was the finest to be had west of the Mississippi River."

"It was wonderfully smooth," he agreed. "I think I had better catch up with Emerald and offer my appreciation."

"She has already departed the train."

Longarm grabbed his own bags. "What time does the westbound Santa Fe head out of here?"

"It should be leaving about six o'clock this evening."

Longarm consulted his fine pocket watch. "That gives me a bit over eight hours to find a way to replace my ticket and money."

"I know you will think of something," the conductor said. "See you on the return trip to Denver!"

Longarm waved good-bye to the man and stepped down from the train. He liked the conductor, but he wished the man could have at least loaned him a few dollars so he could eat and maybe find a poker game where he could win back his money. Failing that, what was he to do other than to send a telegram to Billy Vail and explain his sorry circumstances?

Longarm glanced in both directions, hoping to catch a glimpse of Miss Alexander among the throng of passengers and their greeters, but she was nowhere in sight.

What a pity!

With a deep sigh of regret and dejection, he headed into town, madly trying to think of a way to get back a hundred dollars plus a train ticket. Damn Ordella Jensen! When . . . or if . . . he ever managed to return to Denver, he would catch up with her and give the little hustler a lesson in the merits of honesty!

Longarm trudged into town, wondering what to do next. He was disappointed that he hadn't at least been afforded the opportunity to thank Emerald Alexander for paying their large supper tab. But he supposed she might be so disgusted with him that she never wanted to see his face again.

He stopped in town at a large pawnshop and studied the sign in the window that offered fair cash value.

Through the window, Longarm could see a handsome young customer with his pocket watch and gold chain lying on the counter. Behind the counter was a small man wearing a nightshade and spectacles who was obviously making an offer for the watch. But the customer appeared to get angry and then snatched up his watch and stomped outside.

"Excuse me," Longarm said, intercepting the young man. "I was thinking of pawning something, but you seemed to have had a bad experience inside just now."

The man pulled out his gold pocket watch and chain and dangled them before Longarm's eyes. "You're looking at a pocket watch made by the finest watchmakers in all of Switzerland. This valuable piece was presented to me on my twenty-first birthday by my late father. The chain is gold, and the total value is no less than one hundred dollars in any reputable pawnshop. But do you know what that thief behind the counter had the audacity to offer?"

"I've no idea."

"Fifteen dollars!" The young man's face darkened with outrage. "Why, I'd throw this watch and chain in the river before I'd submit to such an insult!"

"I understand," Longarm said with genuine sympathy. "When a man is down on his luck and fortune, there are those who would quickly take advantage."

"Sir, do you have a watch and chain?"

"I do," Longarm said. "And also a handgun I was hoping to borrow money against."

"He might give you better money on a gun," the young man said. "But I very much doubt it. That money-hungry little fellow inside is a pirate posing as a respectable businessman."

"Such would seem to be the case."

Longarm watched the man hurry away and was about to turn and continue on down the street when the owner of the pawnshop touched his sleeve. "Excuse me?"

"What?" Longarm asked, looking down at the little man with the nightshade and thick eyeglasses.

"My name is Mr. Levi Swartz. I own this pawnshop."

"So I guessed."

"Sir," Swartz said nervously, "forgive me, but I overheard what that young man said to you just now. Meaning no disrespect to him or yourself, I must point out that he was quite inaccurate in his statement."

"How is that?" Longarm asked.

"His pocket watch was a fake."

"What do you mean?"

"I mean that his watch wasn't a *real* Hampton made in Switzerland."

"Oh?"

"It was a fake. Some shyster just engraved that name on the back of the case. And what the young man thought was a solid gold casing was really only thinly plated gold over brass. Furthermore, the watch didn't work and probably had the poorest of inner workings. It was, I'm sad to say, a piece of junk that not even a self-respecting tinhorn gambler would wear."

Swartz sounded convincing, but Longarm wasn't ready to pass judgment yet. "Did that young man explain to you that his late father had presented it to him as a birthday gift?"

"Of course he did!" Swartz cried. "And that's why I just couldn't find it in my heart to tell him the truth of the fraud. I don't know if his father was also cheated or not, but the watch was a fake and the chain was also thinly gold plated."

Longarm found himself believing the pawnshop owner.

49

"I have an Ingersol watch attached to a solid gold chain on one end and a very fine derringer to the other. I know the quality of all three pieces. I'm a United States deputy marshal, and the derringer has saved my life on several occasions."

Levi Swartz took his arm. "Come inside, Marshal! I must assume you are in need of money, and perhaps we can do business."

"Perhaps," Longarm said, but he doubted it as Swartz went behind his counter filled with rings, watches, and other jewelry. Behind the counter in a glass case were at least fifty pistols, a large assortment of rifles, and even some beautifully carved and decorated Indian bows, quivers, and arrows.

Swartz extended his soft little hand. "May I see your Ingersol, chain, and derringer, please?"

Longarm laid them out on the felt-topped counter. Swartz quickly examined all three with an eyepiece and nodded his head. "Excellent quality. But I've never seen a derringer attached to the opposite end of a pocket watch."

"It's proven to be a lifesaver. I keep the watch in one pocket of my vest and the derringer in the other vest pocket. So in a bad fix, I pretend to reach for my watch when, in fact, I'm reaching for the derringer."

"Clever. Very clever. For these, I can give you a good price."

"I don't want to sell them," Longarm told him. "I only want a loan so I can recoup my losses. I have to be on the train for Arizona, and it leaves at six o'clock."

"I see. And how much is the ticket?"

"It will be about twenty-five dollars."

"But you will also need some traveling money."

"Yes," Longarm admitted. "I'm ashamed to say that I

was robbed of one hundred dollars, and I have an assignment to track down a gang of outlaws in Arizona."

Levi Swartz frowned. "Do you have proof that you're a United States marshal?"

Longarm showed the man his badge. "But I can't hock this badge."

"Of course you can't," Swartz said. "The truth is, another federal marshal saved me from being lynched by a drunken mob about three years ago. And for his trouble, he was later ambushed and shot to death. I pray for his soul every day and thank him for my life."

"What was the marshal's name?"

"Jim Baker."

"I knew Marshal Baker very well," Longarm said, his voice hardening. "In fact, we were close friends. And if it's any consolation to you, I tracked down the man who killed him and sent the killer to the gallows."

Tears sprang up behind the pawnshop owner's spectacles, and he had to remove them to dry his eyes. With a voice filled with emotion, he turned, went to a safe, opened it and removed cash, then returned to Longarm, who stood waiting and wondering what would happen next.

"Here is one hundred dollars," Swartz whispered in a voice choking with emotion.

Longarm stared at the stack of bills. "That's a lot to loan on my watch, chain, and derringer."

"Of course it would be," Swartz said. "Far too much to loan. So keep them and consider the one hundred dollars a loan to be repaid with no collateral."

"What?"

"You get this money on the shake of our hands."

Longarm just stared at Levi Swartz. "You don't require anything of value?"

"My life is of value, and your friend saved it at the expense of his own." Swartz extended his hand. "Marshal, I hope and expect you will repay me, but if you don't, then I will not be bitter. A debt will have been repaid."

Longarm took the man's hand and shook it firmly. "Mr. Swartz, I thank you, and I will repay your loan. Write out your address so I can send you the money as soon as possible."

Swartz wrote: Levi Swartz Pawn Brokerage, Santa Fe, New Mexico Territory.

Longarm pocketed his watch, gold chain, and double-barreled derringer. He was touched by this man's trust and sense of obligation but chose not to say much more than a quick thanks for the money and a second promise that it would be repaid.

As Longarm left the pawnshop, he turned to wave a good-bye at the pawn broker but Levi Swartz was gazing off into space with a big smile on his homely little face.

Longarm spent two dollars on a shave and haircut and something to eat and drink. Then, he strolled around the plaza listening to Mexicans play their fiddles and guitars for coins. Later, he sat in the shade of a big acacia tree and enjoyed watching children play a game of tag around the huge plaza fountain. Longarm saw young lovers walking arm in arm across the grass and discovered that he envied them.

He was killing time in the day until he could go to the station and buy another train ticket for Arizona. Given the fact that it would have to come out of the borrowed cash Levi Swartz had generously provided, he would travel third class on the Santa Fe. That was not a big deal, because Longarm was plenty accustomed to those stark and uncomfortable surroundings in which the poor traveled by train. The important thing was to get to Flagstaff and then have enough money to take up after the Grand Canyon Gang.

"Hello, Custis Long," a warm and familiar voice called.

Longarm turned and came to his feet. "Why, if it isn't Miss Emerald Alexander! I'm surprised you would even acknowledge my presence, given that you had to pay for last night's meal and drinks."

"I'm not happy about it, but the conductor explained how you were robbed and I wanted you to know that I understand and you have my sympathy."

Longarm grinned with relief. "I'm very glad to hear that."

"And I'm glad to see that the scabs on your face are almost gone."

He self-consciously touched his face. "Me, too."

"Custis, do you remember that I told you I had some business here in Santa Fe?"

"Yes."

"This business is not going at all well. I wondered if you might be interested in helping me . . . for a fee."

"What do you mean?"

"I am owned a large sum of money by a man here in Santa Fe, and he refuses to pay me."

"Do you have proof of this debt?"

"Of course," Emerald said, reaching into her purse and extracting a piece of paper that she unfolded and handed to Longarm. "The document of debt is quite straightforward."

Longarm read the document carefully. It was a promissory note, notarized by the county recorder for a debt of a thousand dollars to be paid in January to Miss Emerald Alexander. The note was signed by a Mr. Todd Grover.

"Who is this man?" Longarm asked.

"He's a professional here in Santa Fe, an important man who can easily pay me my money but refuses."

"Then perhaps you should see an attorney."

"Mr. Grover *is* an attorney."

Longarm was getting confused. "Then if he knows this debt is due and the document is legal, why is he refusing to pay you the money?"

"Why not? He knows I can't remain here in Santa Fe for weeks while a court date is set and a judge finally hands down his judgment. And even after that, I still might have trouble collecting on my own in this town where he has so many important connections and a great deal of influence."

"Yes, I see."

"If you will collect this debt from Mr. Grover before the train leaves, I will give you . . . a ten percent commission and buy you another first-class ticket on the Santa Fe."

"A hundred dollars off the top and a first-class ticket?"

"Yes. You get the cash from Mr. Grover, take your cut, then give me nine hundred dollars and I buy us both tickets for Arizona. Marshal, time is of the essence. Are you interested in my proposition?"

"Of course. Where is Mr. Grover?"

"His office is in the county courthouse, second floor. His name is on the door in gold lettering. He will be . . . difficult to persuade, and you'll need to be extremely firm."

"Firm is my middle name," Longarm said. "Lead the way."

"I won't go inside the courthouse," Emerald said, lips pursed and tight with anger. "It will be better if I wait outside. If Mr. Grover doesn't have the cash, he'll have a checkbook on his person. Make him write out and sign the check to me for immediate payment. His bank is just across the street."

"You seem to know a lot about Mr. Grover."

"I should," Emerald said, her voice quivering with rage, "because, up until five months ago, Todd was my gawd-damned husband."

Longarm stared, but Emerald either wouldn't or couldn't say another word.

Chapter 6

Longarm wasn't thrilled about twisting some sleazy attorney's arm for the overdue money, but he couldn't think of an easier way to get back a hundred dollars plus a first-class train ticket to Arizona, so he headed across the street to the county courthouse.

He didn't say a word as he mounted the stairs and found the office of Todd Grover, Esquire. Longarm opened the door and stepped inside a well-appointed but uninhabited foyer. The walls were decorated with excellent lithographs by Currier and Ives. The furniture was dark and heavy, and the rug was of the highest quality. It didn't take much to see that Todd Grover was doing very well financially. That was good, because it meant the guy was probably good for the money.

"Hello?" Longarm called, approaching the closed inner office door. "Anyone here?"

He heard a dull thud and supposed it was Grover's feet dropping from his desk to the floor. A moment later, the door opened and Longarm stood face to face with a heavy-set man with dark circles under his eyes. He was of average height but looked dissipated although he could not have been more than thirty-five years old. Todd Grover wore the flushed cheeks of a heavy drinker, but he was well dressed with a diamond stickpin in his tie.

Todd licked his thin lips, tried to force a smile through what was probably a horrendous hangover, and asked, "Can I help you?"

"Yes, you can," Longarm told the man. "I have come in the matter of a debt that is in need of being collected."

"I see. Well, perhaps I can help you collect the debt, and I generally take twenty-five percent, depending on the circumstances." Grover still apparently had no idea that *he* was the debtor. "Come inside Mr. . . ."

"Long. Federal Deputy Marshal Custis Long."

"Impressive," Grover said, not looking at all impressed as he shut the office door so they could speak in absolute privacy. "So who is the deadbeat you need me to file papers against?"

Without directly answering, Longarm unfolded the document that Emerald had given him. "I believe you owe your ex-wife one thousand dollars, and I've come to see that it is paid today."

Longarm had no idea what the attorney's reaction would be, but he was caught completely off guard when the man laughed outright.

"Is something funny, Mr. Grover?"

"You are," the man said, jamming the note into Longarm's chest. "This document isn't worth the paper it is written upon."

"I'm afraid that I disagree. It is perfectly clear to me that you owe your ex-wife one thousand dollars. Look, the note has been properly notarized."

"Can't you even read, you idiot?"

Longarm was not in the habit of being insulted, and his

hand automatically shot out and grabbed Grover by his throat. Then, Longarm heaved the attorney backward so forcefully that the back of Todd Grover's legs struck his desk and he went flying over the top of it, crashing against the wall before he slid to the floor.

Longarm was surprised at the damage he'd done, and he certainly hadn't meant to hurl Grover with such force and perhaps cause him grievous injury.

"Sir," Longarm said, hurrying around behind the desk to help the attorney to his feet. "I didn't mean to hurt you, but the debt . . ."

Longarm's jaw dropped, because Todd Grover was lying on his back with his neck twisted at a very unnatural angle. "Oh my God!" Longarm whispered, dropping to the unconscious man's side and taking his pulse. "Mr. Grover!"

Longarm heard a strangled, gurgling sound and felt so relieved that he almost wept with happiness. "Mr. Grover!" he cried, grabbing the attorney and pulling him away from the wall so his neck was no longer awkwardly bent. "Can you breathe?"

Longarm heard more gurgling, but Grover's eyes did pop open and he tried to speak. His eyes were unfocused, his chest was heaving as if he'd run for miles, and he was having terrible convulsions.

"I'll get a doctor!" Longarm cried, jumping to his feet and racing out the door.

He ran down the upper floor hallway, yelling for help, and when a woman emerged he grabbed her by the shoulders. "There's been an accident. Mr. Grover is hurt and needs a doctor!"

"What on earth happened?"

"He . . . he fell over backward and hit his head against the wall."

"Oh, dear!" the woman screeched. "There's a doctor two blocks down the street. His name is Kelly."

"I'll find and bring him back here," Longarm vowed, racing off without asking which way down the street he should run.

When he came flying out of the courthouse, Emerald intercepted him. "Did you get the thousand dollars I'm owed?"

"Not exactly," Longarm said. "Which way do I go to find Dr. Kelly?"

Emeralds eyes widened. "Good grief, what *did* you do to Todd?"

"I pushed him, and he went over his desk backward and may have sprung his neck. I didn't mean to hurt the man."

"You idiot!"

"Don't call me that!" Longarm bellowed, feeling a rising panic. "And besides, you said I'd have to be very firm."

"I never dreamed you'd attack Todd and break his neck!"

Before Longarm could react, Emerald was racing up the courthouse steps and disappearing into the building. Longarm started running down the street, and when he'd gone two blocks without a sign of Kelly's office, it hit him that he'd gone the wrong direction. Boy, this just wasn't his day! He reversed directions and pounded up the street until he finally found the doctor's office.

A nurse was in the waiting room with three patients. Longarm yelled, "Where's Dr. Kelly?"

Her eyes widened and then cut to a closed door. "He's examining Mrs. Caldwell right now and . . ."

Longarm didn't wait to hear the rest, because this was a life-or-death emergency! He slammed into the doctor's examining room. "Dr. Kelly, there's just been a terrible accident!" he shouted, badly winded and gasping for air.

Kelly was a short but very intelligent-looking doctor who wore a white smock and pressed black trousers. The patient he was bent over examining, Mrs. Caldwell, was an older, matronly, heavy woman. Her dress was pulled up above her waist, and her legs were spread wide apart and supported by two metal arms affixed with leather straps for her ankles. When Longarm saw *what* Dr. Kelly was examining, he almost lost his last meal.

Mrs. Caldwell let out a shriek that could have been heard clear down to the courthouse. Dr. Kelly dropped some metal object he had been using as a probe and roared with indignation.

"Are you crazy? Get out of here this instant!"

Longarm spun around and faced the door. "Look, I'm sorry to have burst in here like this, but Mr. Todd Grover had a terrible accident and he might have broken his neck. You need to come with me right this minute, Dr. Kelly."

"Get him out of here!" Mrs. Caldwell wailed. "Close that door! Everyone is just . . . just staring at my . . . oh, my heavens!"

And then the poor woman fainted.

Dr. Kelly snatched up the shiny probe and hurled it at Longarm. It struck him in the shoulder, but it didn't hurt nearly as bad as the doctor's words. "This is outrageous! I'll have you sued!"

"But Doctor, Mr. Grover is strangling for air. He might die if you don't help him."

"You're the one who will die if you don't shut that door this very instant. I'll be out in a moment!"

Longarm banged the examining room door shut and leaned against it for a moment wondering if his incredibly bad luck was ever going to change. The nurse and the three patients seemed to be frozen with shock.

"Well, damnit," Longarm raged. "You're all grown-ups. It's not like you haven't seen that thing before. So . . . so snap out of it and act normal!"

The four of them were still mute with shock when Longarm stomped out of the doctor's office and headed for the nearest saloon. Either Dr. Kelly would reach attorney Todd Grover in time to save his neck . . . or he would not. But Longarm had done everything he could to save the man. And now, having been twice called an idiot and then a crazy, he decided he would take all the coins in his pocket and use them to buy as much Santa Fe whiskey as the market would bear.

Longarm still wasn't feeling much better a half hour later when the town marshal and one of his deputies entered the saloon with drawn pistols. "Custis Long," the marshal shouted, aiming his gun at Longarm's back, "you're under arrest for aggravated assault and battery."

Longarm tossed down the last of his whiskey and turned slowly. He hated to lie, but he had to save his own neck and besides, if Grover hadn't been a drunkard, he would not have toppled so easily. "Mr. Grover lost his balance and he tripped."

"Tripped!"

"That's right," Longarm repeated. "I was going to shake his hand and he backed up and just . . . tripped."

"All the way across his desk?"

"He fell hard," Longarm said, knowing how ridiculous he sounded. "I immediately gave him aid and then rushed off to find a Dr. Kelly."

"Your story is ridiculous. Raise your hands over your head."

"Look, Marshal," Longarm said, "Todd Grover had a bad accident. Has he recovered?"

"Not fully. In fact, he is still having seizures, and Dr. Kelly has not yet left his side. The man's life is still hanging in the balance."

"I never intended to do him physical harm."

"Intended or not, you seriously harmed the man. If he dies, you will be charged with murder."

"And if he lives?"

"Like I said, aggravated assault." The town marshal's eyes narrowed. "You big, bad federal boys think you can come into a town and run roughshod over our citizens. Well, this time you picked the wrong man. Mr. Todd Grover is one of the pillars of our community and . . ."

"I'd wager anything that the man is close to being dead drunk!"

"Drunk I can't say but dead . . . sure. Ollie, take the man's gun, and make sure he doesn't have any hidden weapons."

"Yes sir, Marshal Lacy."

Ollie was huge. He towered over Longarm, who stood six foot four, and he had the wide, sloping shoulders of an ox. Ollie also had a rather stupid smile on his wide, flat face, giving Longarm the impression that the man was not altogether bright.

"You ain't gonna make me hurt you, are you, mister?"

"No, I'm not," Longarm said. "Take my Colt, but keep your big paws off me. I won't be manhandled by anyone."

Ollie glanced over his shoulder toward Marshal Lacy, who nodded to go ahead and do as he'd been told. A moment later, Longarm was disarmed and being led out of the saloon. By now, a large crowd of curious onlookers had gathered, and one of them was Emerald Alexander.

"Emerald," Longarm called. "Help me out here!"

"Who are you?"

"What?"

"Sir," Emerald said, "I have no idea who you are or why you have attacked my poor husband."

"Emerald!"

Longarm was so enraged that he might even have attacked Emerald if Ollie hadn't chosen that moment to give him a hard shove in the back of the head.

So instead of Emerald, Longarm pivoted around and buried his fist in the stupid deputy's stomach. He might as well have slugged a bull in the ribs for all the good his effort did. Ollie drew back his own fist, and fired a straight right cross at Longarm's jaw. It was a punch that would have dropped a horse, but it took about five seconds, and by that time, Longarm was hammering hard, swift blows to Ollie's iron jaw and the giant was beginning to buckle at the knees.

Longarm would have dropped big Ollie in the dust if he'd had time for about three more uppercuts, but Marshal Lacy ended the fight with the barrel of his gun.

The next thing Longarm knew, he was tumbling head over heels down a deep, dark well.

When Longarm awoke his head was ringing like a great mission bell, and when he tried to climb off the louse-infested bunk in his jail cell, he gasped with pain.

"So," Marshal Lacy said, "you really are a federal officer."

Longarm's hand went to his side, and he discovered that Lacy had not only relieved him of his badge and revolver, but also his watch, chain, and derringer. "Yeah, I'm a federal officer. And I'll tell you something, Lacy, I don't much appreciate the way this has been handled. I want out of this jail cell immediately."

"Can't do it. You see, Marshal Long, you almost did kill Mr. Grover."

"So he's alive, is he?"

"That's right."

"It's his word against mine as to what happened in his office."

"Dr. Kelly says there are bruises caused by fingerprints all over the attorney's throat."

Longarm swallowed hard. "Oh yeah?"

"That's right. And while I might be skeptical of what Todd Grover has to say . . . not that I'm calling him a liar, but he does bend the truth at times . . . Dr. Kelly *never* lies. He has no reason to do so."

"I see," Longarm said, feeling his own throat constrict with worry.

"You want to tell me what really happened in the office and why you were there?"

"I went to collect one thousand dollars from Mr. Grover for his ex-wife, Miss Emerald Alexander."

"Impossible."

Exasperated, Longarm shouted, "Did you happen to find the promissory note? I had it in my possession when I went into the man's office. It was even notarized, but in my haste to get a doctor, I dropped it on the floor."

"There was no note in Mr. Grover's office."

"But there had to be!"

"Sorry."

"Look again, Marshal. You'll see that I'm telling the truth."

"Marshal Long, I *did* look. No note. Mr. Grover was unconscious when Dr. Kelly arrived, and I even asked the doctor but he didn't see any documents laying around, either."

Longarm gripped the cell bars. "Then someone took the

note and . . . it must have been Emerald who found and picked it up!"

"You mean the woman you claim was Grover's ex-wife?"

"That's right."

"No," the marshal said, "that's wrong. You see, Todd Grover's wife and childhood sweetheart died four years ago."

"What!"

"She's buried in the town cemetery, Marshal Long. And if you ever get out of my jail, you can go and see her grave for yourself. You might even lay red roses on it for all I care."

Longarm had to sit down on his bunk. "Then the whole story Emerald told me was a fabrication. Her promissory note was a forgery and a fraud. And I was sent up to Mr. Grover's office to extort one thousand dollars from him that he probably never even owed."

The marshal of Santa Fe nodded his head in agreement. "Not only did you assault and almost break Mr. Grover's neck, but you assaulted my deputy. Two assault charges will get you some serious time in my jail—perhaps even in our territorial prison."

"Oh man," Longarm groaned. "When it rains it pours. Could I borrow a pen and pencil?"

"What for?"

"I need to send a telegram to Denver."

"Yeah, I can see that you might. Got any money left to send it?"

Longarm searched his pockets in vain. "Nope."

Marshal Lacy sighed. "All right. Make it a real short telegram, and I'll foot the bill."

"Thanks."

"Marshal Long, you've had a *real* bad day. I suggest

you lie down and catch some sleep. You haven't been thinking very well, and maybe sleep will change that . . . but I doubt it. Given either your stupidity or extreme bad judgment, how did you ever become a federal marshal?"

"I'm beginning to wonder," Longarm said feeling devastated and betrayed. "Has the westbound Santa Fe left yet?"

"Yes, it has."

It didn't matter. Emerald was gone, and he, the dupe, was in deep trouble and bound for a long jail sentence. Still, he could not resist asking, "I don't suppose you know if Emerald Alexander or whatever her real name is boarded the westbound train."

"As a matter of fact, she did. I sent Ollie to the Santa Fe depot to collect a package. He said he saw the woman get onboard, and she never looked back."

"No," Longarm said bitterly, "she wouldn't have."

He stretched out on his bunk and tried to think of what he could possibly do next to mess up his life. But, given his miserable circumstances, the possibilities were quite limited. And having nothing better to do with his life, Longarm closed his eyes, hoping he could sleep right on through until tomorrow with a new day and better luck.

Chapter 7

Longarm did sleep until the next day, when Ollie, with lumps all over his lantern jaw, banged on the jail bars and shouted, "Wake up! Breakfast is ready!"

Longarm rolled off his bunk and knuckled the sleep from his eyes. "Your face looks like you've been whipped pretty good, Ollie. Or maybe you're so forgetful you think you ran into walls while you sleepwalked last night."

"You caught me by surprise with those quick punches," Ollie said, looking more insulted than angry. "No man ever did that before, and it won't happen again."

"It would if you tried to rough me up," Longarm told the huge deputy. "I hope you're faster with a pistol than you are with your fists."

Ollie touched his lumpy and swollen jaw. "You loosened three of my front teeth."

"Sorry."

"And I don't use a pistol. I use a rifle, and I can shoot the eye out of a crow at fifty paces."

"Is that a fact?"

"Yep. I'm a deadeye shot with a rifle."

"I'd never have guessed you had any worthwhile talents."

The insult went right over Ollie's domed head, and he said proudly, "The reason I'm so good with a rifle is that Pa didn't allow me but one shot to bring home the meat. If I used it and missed, I got whupped real bad. So I got real good with a rifle. Better'n you, I bet."

"I'm glad to hear that. Where is your marshal?"

"He went to send that telegram to Billy Vail like you asked. Is Vail gonna come all the way down here and try to save your bacon?"

"I don't know."

"He can't, you know. Marshal Lacy says that, most likely, you're going to the territorial prison."

"So I hear."

"I'll bet there are men in them prisons that will whup up on you every day, you havin' been a federal marshal and all. I hear them fellas in prison are meaner than a pack of wild dogs. I sure wouldn't want to go there if I were you."

"I usually manage to take care of myself."

Ollie shrugged. "You couldn't whup all them bad prisoners. Not every day, you couldn't. Even I couldn't do it. No sir!"

Longarm was already bored with this conversation. "How long have you been Lacy's deputy?"

"Two years."

"And you're still alive? Amazing."

Ollie frowned. "Why is that?"

"Because you just don't seem like you're cut out to be a lawman."

"And you are?" Ollie hooted with laughter. "Me and Marshal Lacy been sayin' you're the dumbest federal marshal we ever heard of!"

Longarm's cheeks turned hot with humiliation, but he held his tongue.

"I mean, how could you be so stupid as to whup up on Mr. Grover, who knows most everything there is to know about the law? And worse yet, you let some woman trick you!"

"I must have had my fool's cap on yesterday, Ollie. But this is a whole new day, and I'm thinking a lot clearer."

"Sure," Ollie said, "but you can think clear all you want in that cell. Ain't goin' to do you a bit of good 'cause you already done messed up everything for your stupid self."

Longarm decided that Ollie wasn't quite as dense as he first appeared. Still, he was in no mood to be taunted, and the insult was close enough to the truth that it rankled. "Ollie, leave me alone."

"Marshal Lacy says you'll get extra time for hittin' me."

"Is that right?"

"It sure is. I saw Mr. Grover, and he says he's gonna make sure you go to prison so long your hair will turn white and your pecker will shrink to the size of a termite."

"Todd Grover said that?"

"He did! That man is sure mad at you. He says that, after you hit him, you robbed him of four hundred dollars and his pocket watch."

"No!"

"Yep."

"I didn't take a thing of Grover's. If I had, where is his money and watch? I sure haven't got them hidden on my body."

"Maybe you hid Grover's stuff somewhere after you ran out of his office and ended up in the Acme Saloon."

"If I had four hundred dollars stashed away I'd be asking a judge to free me on bail."

"Oh," Ollie said, hanging both thumbs in his worn-out britches, "you could do that, but Judge Potter wouldn't let you get out of here for any amount of bail."

"And why not?"

" 'Cause he's Mr. Grover's father-in-law."

Longarm shook his head and silently damned his continuing run of bad luck. "Well, then, I guess my goose is just cooked, Ollie."

"I guess it is. Too bad. I hear that federal lawmen make a lot more money than us locals."

"I wouldn't know."

"I only make twenty dollars a month. How much do you make?"

"A little more."

"A *lot* more, I'll bet!" Ollie winked. "I'll bet you make at least fifty dollars a month."

Actually, that was about what Longarm was making, but he hadn't started out making that much money. "Starting wages for a deputy marshal are around thirty-five dollars a month, but we can make a bit more if we travel."

"See! That's a *lot* more money than I earn."

"My job is more dangerous, Ollie."

"I'd like to have your job," Ollie announced. "Do you think, after you go to prison, I could have your job?"

"I don't know," Longarm said.

"I might go to Denver and ask for your job."

"I think you ought to stay right here in Santa Fe."

"You're only saying that because you're still hopin' for some way out of getting sent to prison and getting the shit beat out of you every day. That's why you don't want me after your job."

"Right."

Longarm couldn't bear to continue this inane conversation another moment, so he went back to his bunk and lay down facing the wall. Now there was nothing to do but wait for word from his friend and boss, Billy Vail. And given that Billy didn't brook much in the way of his deputies getting in fixes, there was no telling what the man would do or say to help Longarm.

Billy Vail did receive the telegram, and the one he immediately sent back to Santa Fe was remarkable in its brevity. It read: INFORM YOUR JUDGE THAT I WILL ARRIVE IN SANTA FE THE DAY AFTER TOMORROW TO GET DEPUTY LONG'S BAIL.

Marshal Lacy showed Longarm the one-sentence telegram and added, "Your boss might think he can ride in here on a white charger and save your ass, but Judge Potter won't hear of it. There's nothing your boss can do to keep you from going to prison."

"We'll see," Longarm told the man. "I can tell you that if I get set free, you and Ollie are in for a lot of disappointment."

"Won't happen," Lacy promised, "what with Mr. Grover being an attorney and the judge being his father-in-law. Your goose is as good as cooked."

"We'll see," Longarm said, trying to sound confident despite his lack of optimism.

Billy was a persuasive man, but to Longarm, it didn't seem that any amount of persuasion would be able to get him free of two assault charges plus the bogus charge of stealing Todd Grover's watch and four hundred dollars.

"Ollie says he wants your job."

"I told him to forget about it."

"That's what I told him," Marshal Lacy admitted. "Ollie is a good man. Now, I'm not saying he's real bright, but he more than makes up for that in his loyalty and bravery. Ollie would run through a plateglass window if I gave him that order."

"So I gathered." Longarm frowned. "Is Ollie married with children?"

"No, he's a confirmed bachelor. I don't think he's ever even kissed a girl, although he'd sure like to. Why do you ask?"

"Because he should not be a lawman. In fact, I'll go even further than that and say I think he's going to get himself killed or hurt one of these days."

Instead of arguing, Marshal Lacy turned and went over to his desk, looking worried.

"Did you hear me?" Longarm asked.

"I heard you all right. And I'm of the same mind."

"Then why don't you do Ollie a favor and fire him?"

"Because," Lacy said, "it would just plumb break his heart. You see, his father was a lawman in his younger days. As he got old and then started dying, he asked that his son follow in his footsteps. Ollie's father was his hero."

"That might be, but I'd hate to see Ollie follow his father to an early grave. A man that big and strong ought to be a farmer."

"Yeah, except he's got no money to buy a farm."

"Then a blacksmith or a muleskinner."

"Ollie's fingers are so big he couldn't hold horseshoe nails without dropping them. And the man is deathly afraid of mules. One kicked him in the head when he was fifteen."

"That explains a lot," Longarm said, going back to his bunk. "And by the way, I want to have a talk with Mr. Grover."

"Well, he doesn't want to see you until it's time to go to court."

"Marshal, I never took the man's watch or money! I'm a United States deputy marshal, for hell's sake!"

Lacy frowned. "To tell you the truth, I don't think you took Grover's watch or money, either. But someone might have during the time he was strangling and unconscious."

"I think the woman I arrived with on the train and who set me up for the trouble I'm in took Grover's money and watch. I think she probably even took my federal traveling money and train ticket!"

"I wouldn't know about that. At any rate, the woman is gone, and we'll never know for sure if she was a thief."

"I'll find her in Arizona," Longarm vowed. "She played me for the fool and is the one responsible for getting me in this terrible fix."

"I hope your boss is bringing a satchel full of federal dollars," Lacy said.

"Why is that?"

"Because just between you and me and the cell bars, Grover can be bought and so can his father-in-law, Judge Potter."

"You don't say."

"I did say, but I'll deny it if you repeat my words. I'm only telling you this because you are a lawman and I'd hate to see you sent to prison. Those boys down there hate lawmen with an undying passion, and they'd kill you."

Longarm had nothing to say about that. And as far as Billy Vail was concerned, he didn't think the man would try to bribe anyone. Billy had a code of honor, and it didn't include paying off corrupt judges and lawyers.

Well, Longarm thought, *I got nothing to do but lie here on this stinking bunk and wait to see which way the chips are going to fall.*

Chapter 8

When Marshal Billy Vail climbed down from the train in Santa Fe, he was in a grim frame of mind. He had been desk-bound so long in the Denver federal building that he'd forgotten how uncomfortable and inconvenient it was to travel great distances. Furthermore, the train had broken down on the Raton Pass, and he'd been stranded there with the other second-class passengers for more than eight mind-numbing hours. Then, they'd run out of food, and Billy was a man who liked his food—great quantities of it. He and the other famished passengers had been saved from starvation by some Ute Indians who sold them jerky at outrageous prices.

The last straw had been when he'd tripped climbing back onboard the train at Raton Pass, fallen, and badly bruised his knees while also ruining his suit pants. A man with holes in the knees of his pants just didn't feel that good about himself. And so now, hungry, limping, and too long without sleep, Marshal Billy Vail had to face the daunting task of trying to extricate his favorite deputy from one hell of a muddled mess.

"Where is the marshal's office?" Billy demanded of the porter who was standing at the depot in Santa Fe.

"Just up the street and off the plaza on San Francisco Street," the man said. "It's an adobe with a big sign out front. You can't miss it."

"Where's the best hotel in town?"

"I'd suggest the Hotel Conch." The porter's eyes dropped down to the holes in Billy's pants and then he added, "However, there are quite a few more modestly priced hotels that you might want to stay at if you are low on money."

Billy followed the man's eyes to his torn trousers, and he knew what the porter was thinking—this man didn't qualify to stay in the Hotel Conch.

"The Hotel Conch sounds good," he snapped, grabbing his bags and heading up the street.

Billy wanted to go first to the marshal's office but thought better of that idea. Mostly, he wanted to wait to face the marshal because he was the kind of man who believed that first impressions were critical in the success of any difficult undertaking. If your opponents sized you up as weak or unworthy, they treated you with disdain. Billy wanted respect, so he found the finest clothing store in Santa Fe and ordered a new suit. Because he was short and stocky, there were alterations to be made to the length of the sleeves and pants, but the tailor assured Billy that his new and expensive suit would be ready in two hours and delivered to his room at the Hotel Conch.

Billy paid the man a price that was less than he would have had to pay for the same quality in Denver and checked into Santa Fe's best hotel. He overlooked the skeptical glance of the desk clerk, was insulted when he was asked to pay a night's lodging in advance, but did so and then went and had a hot bath and fresh shave.

It was nearly five o'clock when Billy, shoes shined by a boy in the hotel's lobby, finally stood before a huge mirror and deemed himself impressive and presentable in his newly tailored suit of clothes. Confident of his appearance, he headed straight for the marshal's office. Minutes later, he barged in without knocking and immediately saw Longarm stretched out on a thin mattress in a ridiculously small jail cell. Closer, he saw a sloppy-looking marshal and a giant deputy sleeping with their feet resting on their desks.

"Good afternoon!" Billy boomed, jarring both the lawmen from their afternoon nap. "I am United States Marshal William Vail, and I've come to get my deputy out of this jail. Furthermore, I'm damned upset and assure you both that I will conduct a full and complete investigation into this outrage."

Marshal Lacy rubbed his eyes and yawned. Ollie, however, blurted, "I'd sure like to be a federal marshal, sir. I can shoot the eye out of a crow at a hundred yards with a Winchester, and when I punch a man he stays down for the count."

"So what?" Billy challenged, dismissing both lawmen as he marched over to stand before the cell. "Custis, how do you manage to do these things?"

"Howdy, Billy. You have a nice train trip down here?" Longarm asked, slowly climbing to his feet.

"It was wretched! Custis, you've gotten yourself in a real pickle this time."

"I'm afraid so."

"What happened?"

In as few words as possible, Longarm explained how his affairs since leaving Denver had managed to go from bad to worse. He ended up by saying, "Mr. Todd Grover, in addition to assault, is also accusing me of the theft of his watch and four hundred dollars."

"That's ridiculous!"

"Sure it is," Longarm said, "but that's what the shyster is claiming. And either he's lying or he was robbed by someone else—probably Emerald."

"Women are going to be the death of you yet."

"Could be. You gonna go my bail, Billy?"

"Do I have any choice?"

"I expect so," Longarm replied, "but getting me out of this place would be greatly appreciated—and the sooner the better. I wouldn't feed *hogs* the slop they bring me to eat."

"I might not be able to get you out on bail until tomorrow." Billy scowled. "And I suppose you lost your travel money again?"

"It was stolen," Longarm said, looking pained. "At first I thought Ordella was the thief and that she'd fleeced me just before I boarded the train out of Denver. Now, however, I'm pretty sure it was Emerald that not only took my money and train ticket, but is responsible for all my troubles here in Santa Fe."

"Not all of them," Billy said, lips tightly pursed. "You're plenty responsible enough for your own miseries."

"Billy," Longarm said, "I'm having a real tough time in here. That big, dumb deputy over there named Ollie seems to take some kind of sick delight in reminding me every few hours about how I'm going to be murdered in the New Mexico Territorial Prison."

Billy shot Ollie a withering look, and the giant managed to offer a weak, inoffensive smile. Then, Billy turned to the marshal and said, "I want my deputy to be fed a big steak tonight with potatoes and pie for dessert."

"Sorry, Marshal Vail, but a fancy meal like that ain't in our budget."

Billy removed his wallet, laid down five dollars on the marshal's desk, and said, "Use this to buy Custis a steak dinner and his breakfast. He's skinnier than when he left Denver, so I know you've been feeding him poorly."

"Your marshal is a damned finicky eater."

"Feed him what I've paid you for. Now, where is your local judge to be found?"

"Most likely in the Blue Diamond Saloon. You'll find it across the plaza."

"He hasn't been here all that long, has he?" Billy asked.

"Five years."

"More like four," Billy said.

Lacy frowned. "How would you know that?"

"I like to know in advance who I'm dealing with. And what I've learned is that Judge Potter is a hard man to deal with."

"He's tough, all right," Marshal Lacy agreed. "I've seen him sentence a man to the gallows for stealing nothing but a sheep."

"Is that a fact?"

"Sure is." Lacy smiled. "My bet is that you'll have to really grease his palm, if you know what I mean, before he lets your man out of my jail."

"I know what you mean," Billy said, his expression hardening.

Billy turned to Longarm. "Eat well, and I'll do whatever it takes to get you out of that rat trap."

"Thanks, boss."

"Don't mention it."

Ollie jumped to his feet and said, "Marshal Vail, if you can't get your man out of going to prison, I'd like to offer my services as his replacement."

Billy looked confused. "What?"

"I'd like to become your federal deputy marshal," Ollie declared, drawing himself up to his full six foot six inches and pushing out his barrel chest. "Like I said, I can shoot straight and punch hard."

Billy tried to walk around the giant, but Ollie slid sideways, blocking his exit. "Sir, my pa was a lawman, one of the best until he was ambushed."

"How about that."

"It was my pa's dying wish that I follow in his footsteps, but mostly all I do here in Old Santa Fe is knock out the town drunks and jail 'em. I'm good at that, but it don't pay well and I'm ready for something more important."

"Ollie," Marshal Lacy said with a look of disgust, "give it up. Marshal Vail has had a long trip down from Denver, and this isn't the time or the place to be bothering him about a federal lawman's job. Besides, don't I treat you better than anyone else in this town?"

"Oh, yes sir!" Ollie said quickly. "And I mean no offense to you or this town, but I am ready for bigger things. I want to be a *federal* officer."

Billy shook his head, placed his hand on the giant's arm, and gently moved him aside so he could pass through the door. "I'll keep you in mind, Ollie."

"Thank you sir! I wouldn't let you down like Marshal Long did."

"I'm sure you wouldn't," Billy said. At the door, he turned and shouted, "Custis, I'll try to get you out of here no later than tomorrow morning."

"I'm countin' on it!" Longarm yelled back. "And thanks for the steak dinner tonight."

"You're welcome," Billy said, shaking his head as he turned and headed off to find the local judge who was already imbibing at the Blue Diamond Saloon.

The saloon was elegant by western standards. It had a long, polished bar along the south wall that would have rivaled almost any in Denver. At least fifty crystal chandeliers were hanging from a ceiling of stamped copper, and the walls were covered with original oils, most of them tending to depict bare-breasted, buxom beauties in rather suggestive poses. The floor was not sawdust like you would find in a lower-class establishment, but instead mahogany. Behind the bar was a fine collection of vintage firearms, including a blunderbuss that Billy would have loved to own. All the walls were painted a stunning blue color, and the curtains matched.

Even the pair of bartenders were resplendent in suits, starched shirts, and collars with diamond-blue ties. All in all, the first impression Billy had was that this was a saloon more suited to Chicago or New York than Santa Fe.

"Good afternoon, sir," a bartender said. "What is your pleasure?"

"Beer," Billy told the man. "Your best, please."

"Very good."

When the beer was brought to Billy, it was in a clean, cold mug. Billy held the glass up to the light of the window and noted that the beverage had a deep, amber color. He tasted and then smacked his lips with approval. "Where does this come from?"

"We have our own brewery," the bartender said with pride. "The barley and hops are imported from the plains of eastern Colorado."

"It's excellent." Billy took another drink, wiped his lips, and said, "Which of these gentlemen here would be Judge Marsden Potter?"

The bartender pointed to a man in his fifties with gray

hair and bushy black eyebrows that matched his mustache. "That is Judge Potter."

"Thank you."

Billy Vail picked up his beer and went over to the judge, who was sitting at a table with two other well-dressed gentlemen.

"Sir?" Billy said. "My name is William Vail, United States Marshal Vail. Excuse me for this interruption, but I have traveled all the way from Denver to see you."

"What on Earth for?"

"It is a private matter. Would it be possible to speak to you alone for a few minutes?"

Marsden Potter excused himself from the company of his companions, and when he stood, Billy realized that the man was already a bit tipsy with drink. He had to grab the edge of his chair and carefully steady himself before walking.

"This had better be important, and it had better not be about that federal officer we have jailed," Potter growled as they moved to the bar.

Billy drained his glass and ordered another round— whiskey for Potter, beer for himself. Then, he leaned close to the judge and said, "My deputy marshal, Custis Long, should not be incarcerated in the local jail."

Potter stiffened and tried to look insulted. In a voice filled with indignation, he said, "I believe your man committed *several* grievous crimes here in Santa Fe and that you are out of order. It will be my determination concerning his guilt or innocence and mine alone!"

"Judge," Billy said, "I understand that you claim to have graduated from the Boston College School of Law."

"What has that to do with anything?"

"Is it true?"

"Of course it's true!"

"Interesting," Billy said. "Before leaving Denver, I sent a telegram to Boston. According to their city magistrate, there is no Boston College School of Law."

"What?"

"You heard me, Judge. Furthermore, there never has been such a school of law."

"This is outrageous!"

"Yes, isn't it though?"

Billy looked around, and every eye in the Blue Diamond Saloon was fixed on them. "Judge, it might be in *your* best interest to step outside where we can find a place to talk without being overheard."

"Sir, you are treading on very shaky ground!"

"And you, Judge, are treading on extremely thin ice. Finish your whiskey and I'll finish my beer, then let's take a short walk."

The judge opened his mouth to utter some other objection, but when his eyes met Billy's, he changed his mind and drained his full glass of whiskey.

Billy took the man's arm and firmly escorted him toward the front door. They made their way into the plaza and found an empty bench under the shade of a tree.

"You didn't graduate from a law school, Judge. You learned what you know from self-study with books. Furthermore, I very much doubt that your real name is Marsden Potter."

"Are you calling me a fraud and a liar?"

"No sir," Billy said, raising his hands, palms outward. "I am just saying that you became a judge here in Santa Fe under circumstances other than what you stated when you applied for the position. And I believe that, given enough time . . . say three or four days . . . I can substantiate those opinions."

The judge snorted. "I have never liked interference

from the feds. This is the Territory of New Mexico in which I am legally authorized to hold court!"

"Authorized by whom?"

"By the territorial governor!"

"Ah yes," Billy said. "That would be Mr. Patrick W. Jamison, an old friend of our Colorado governor who is a friend of mine. I wonder if I can expose your deception with one telegram . . . or if it will take two. And I wonder what Governor Jamison will say about being misled. I'll make sure the Santa Fe newspaper gets its facts straight on you and your appointment."

"You wouldn't do that!"

"Oh, but I would," Billy assured him. "And that's not all. Your son-in-law, Todd Grover, has accused my deputy of grand larceny."

"That is correct."

"No," Billy said slowly, "it isn't. Custis Long would *never* steal. Did Marshal Lacy find the watch and cash that were missing?"

"No, but . . ."

"Judge," Billy said, almost as a parent might say to a child caught with his hand in a cookie jar. "We both know that this whole thing is a deception that I suspect either Mr. Grover created or else he really was robbed but by someone else."

Judge Potter was beginning to sweat. He wiped his hands across his face and swallowed as if he were dying of thirst. "Listen," he croaked, "maybe we can just reach some kind of settlement here."

"You mean like a cash settlement from me to you?"

"Exactly!"

But Billy shook his head. "I'm afraid that would be impossible."

"But why?"

"Because that's not the way I do business," Billy told the man. "What I want and what I expect is for you to tell Marshal Lacy to release Marshal Long. Furthermore, I want all his personal possessions returned to him, and I want you to resign your position as judge."

The man's eyes widened as if he'd seen a ghost. "Never!"

Billy shrugged as if the matter were not of great importance to him. "Judge, either you resign and go away to practice law someplace else, or you will soon be behind bars for fraud. It's really that simple."

Potter's hands began to shake. "You are bluffing."

Billy stood up from the bench. "Then call my bluff or else I shall go to the telegraph office and start the wheels in motion up in Denver."

"Alright!" Potter jumped to his feet. "But give me a week to settle my affairs, to come up with some reason why I must leave Santa Fe."

"You've got three days from the moment my deputy is released to resign."

Potter groaned. "Do you realize that you've just destroyed my life?"

"A life based on deception is a life without merit." Billy toed the dirt. "If you were a good judge, you would never have believed that my deputy marshal, Custis Long, should have been jailed on the mere accusation of theft without any proof. Potter, has your brain become so soaked with alcohol and your palm so accustomed to pay-off money that you've forgotten that a man is innocent until proven guilty?"

Potter blanched and tried to speak, but words failed him completely. Finally, he whirled around and headed back to the Blue Diamond.

Billy shook his head, knowing that he had just destroyed the man's life. Oh, perhaps he could fool someone in a small town and become their magistrate, but whatever position Potter achieved would never equal the importance of the one he was being forced to vacate.

"Too bad," Billy said, not overly proud of what he had just done to the man. "But the truth *is* the truth."

Chapter 9

Of all the things Longarm hated, being jerked around by an imbecile ranked right at the top of his list. And that was exactly what was happening as he sat in his jail cell listening to Deputy Ollie Swenson. The huge deputy had pulled a chair over beside the jail cell at dinnertime and watched Longarm demolish his steak.

"The thing is," Ollie confided, leaning close to the jail cell and drooling over the smell of the steak, "I know who that woman who told you to go into Mr. Grover's office really was. She was real pretty, but she lied to you and is the one who really stole Mr. Grover's watch and money."

"I expect that's true," Longarm said noncommittally. "So who is Emerald if not Todd Grover's ex-wife?"

"Oh, she was married to Mr. Grover, but that was some time ago."

"Before she went to Arizona?"

Ollie frowned as if contemplating some great and deep mystery. "Well," he said evasively, "let's just say that who she really is *now* and *where* she is must be kind of important to you."

"I sure would like to find her," Longarm agreed. "So why don't you just stop trying to be clever . . . which you ain't . . . and tell me where Emerald Alexander went after getting on the westbound train."

"She went to Arizona."

"I already know that! But exactly *where* in Arizona?"

Ollie steepled his fingers. "I wish I could show you what a great shot I am."

"Now why on Earth would I care about that?" Longarm asked, annoyed at the sudden change of subject.

"Because maybe then you'd let me be your assistant United States deputy marshal. And if I became your assistant, you'd soon see that I'm a man born to be a federal lawman. My pa always wanted to be a federal lawman, but he could never get hisself hired."

"I wonder why?" Longarm asked, figuring it was because Ollie's father was as stupid as his giant son.

"Lots of reasons," Ollie answered, looking away with a pained expression. "So Marshal Long, if I was to quit my job here as deputy and become your federal assistant, would you take me along to Arizona?"

"Nope."

"Why not?" Ollie demanded. "I'd be a good assistant, and I'd probably even save your life."

"I don't have the authority to hire you."

"Does Mr. Vail?"

"Yes."

Ollie brightened. "Then I guess I'm speaking to the wrong federal officer."

Ollie started to leave, but Longarm called out, "Wait a minute."

"What?" Ollie asked.

"Do you really know where I can find Emerald Alexander?"

"Sure do." Ollie grabbed the cell bars with his massive hands. "But I won't tell you until I'm wearing a United States Marshal's badge and we get to Arizona. That's my deal, and you can take it . . . or leave it."

Longarm wondered if Billy would deputize Ollie Swenson as a federal marshal for a trip to Arizona. If so, the man might actually be of some help in finding Emerald and helping him retrieve his lost travel money.

"Alright," Longarm said, "show me your quick draw."

"I told you before that I'm not very quick but that I can shoot straight."

"A slow lawman could end up a dead lawman."

"I might be able to get faster," Ollie said. "Watch!"

To Longarm's amazement, Ollie's huge paw dropped to the gun at his side and then he drew the weapon from his holster.

"How was that?"

"I've seen slower, but the fella was pushin' ninety years old."

"Well," Ollie said, looking crestfallen, "I just ain't built for speed. But I hit what I aim for about every time. And I mean to become a federal officer with a pay raise if it's the last thing I ever do."

"It might be if you came to Arizona and step into the trouble I've been sent to clean up near the Grand Canyon."

Ollie dropped his chin to his chest for a moment, then raised it and said, "My pa always told me that being fast is good but being accurate is a lot more important. See that big spider on the wall over yonder?"

Longarm's eyes followed Ollie's pointed finger, and he saw the spider. It was a daddy longlegs and one of the biggest Longarm had ever seen. "Yeah."

"Take a good look at him, 'cause that sucker is history!" Ollie swore, flipping his Colt up and firing.

Longarm couldn't believe the idiot would fire his gun in the middle of the office, but Ollie did . . . and the spider was gone with nothing but a hole in the wall to take his place.

"Damn," Longarm said. "That was pretty good shooting."

"Weren't nothin', Marshal Long. See that fly restin' on that old yellow Wanted poster?"

"I do."

"He's crawlin' down the paper, and I'll drill him as he steps on the wanted man's right eye."

Despite himself, Longarm was fascinated. The distance was only about twenty feet, but the fly was a tiny moving target.

Ollie dropped the gun to his side, tensed, and just as the fly crossed the wanted man's eye, Ollie whipped up the Colt and drilled the insect, leaving a hole where there had been an insect and an eyeball.

"Damn!" Longarm exclaimed. "I'm not too sure I could have hit that fly myself."

Ollie beamed. "I've won plenty of money in shooting contests here in Santa Fe. Ain't but one man ever beat me with a pistol . . . and he's dead now. None ever done it with a Winchester. So do you think I might be a good assistant deputy marshal?"

Longarm sized up the span of the man's shoulders and his huge, muscular arms. The Santa Fe deputy looked like he could pick up a horse and carry it across the street. "Well, Ollie," he said, "you made a believer out of me. But like I told you, I'm just a deputy marshal myself. Marshal Vail is the one who has the authority to hire you on a trail basis."

"Will you tell him how good I am with a gun?"

"I'll tell him," Longarm promised. "But I should also tell you that I'm being sent to Arizona to bring down the Grand Canyon Gang. There's a bunch of them, and they're said to be ruthless and bloody. If you go with me, you'll be putting your life on the line. We'll be going against some tough thieves and murderers."

"I ain't afraid of no Grand Canyon Gang," Ollie scoffed.

"And," Longarm emphasized, "you'd have to help me find Emerald Alexander."

Ollie holstered his gun and crossed his heart in a gesture that was simple yet kind of touching. It convinced Longarm that, although the man might be lacking brainpower, he was sincere, honest, and could be trusted in the toughest of circumstances.

"Alright," Longarm said, making his decision, "I'll talk to Billy and see if we can get you a temporary appointment as my Assistant Deputy United States Marshal."

Ollie's chest swelled up as big as that of a bull buffalo, and he grinned from ear to ear. "Thanks a heap!"

It was about nine o'clock in the evening when Billy finally got around to visiting the jail. Longarm was asleep on his thin cot, and Ollie was sawing logs at his desk.

"Custis," Billy said, tiptoeing past the slumbering giant. "I'm getting you out of there first thing in the morning."

"That's great news."

"Did you get a big steak dinner earlier this evening?"

"I did," Longarm told his boss. "It was sure appreciated. But how'd you manage to get me out of this mess with Judge Potter and Todd Grover?"

"Long, complicated story," Billy answered. He glanced over at Ollie. "That sure is a huge man, and he snores louder than a locomotive huffing at the station."

"Billy," Longarm said. "I lost all my travel money. I'm almost certain that it was stolen from me by a woman named Emerald Alexander, although that might not be her real name. She's also the one who got me in the mess with Grover."

"I brought you more travel money, but you're going to have to make up the loss to the government."

"All of it?"

"Some," Billy hedged. "But if you're successful in Arizona, we can maybe overlook the mess you've made of things so far."

"Oh, I'll take care of the trouble in Arizona," Longarm vowed. "But there is one other thing I need to ask as a favor."

"What?" Billy said, not looking too pleased.

Longarm then told his boss about Deputy Swenson and how he had always wanted to be a federal law officer. He also told Billy that Ollie could help him not only with the Grand Canyon Gang, but also in bringing Emerald to justice.

"He's dumb as an ox but also every bit as strong as one," Longarm said. "And he's as accurate with a six-gun as anyone you'd ever meet. I'd like you to make him my assistant deputy, Billy."

"Forget it!"

"I'll even pay his wages until I've taken care of the trouble in Arizona."

"Pay his wages? Lordy, Custis, how will you do that when you're always getting your money stolen?"

"Billy," Longarm said, "I have a feeling that Ollie Swenson could be a huge help to me."

Billy stared through the bars at him. "Custis, you've never shown any fear or hesitation when given an assignment. Are you all right?"

"Of course I am! But sometimes a man can use a strong right arm. And to be honest, I sort of like that big Swede. So how about it?"

"I guess I could deputize him."

"Only one problem."

"What is that?" Billy asked suspiciously.

"Ollie will insist on a *real* federal marshal's badge."

Billy's fingers absently moved to his chest where his own badge was pinned under his coat. "You aren't suggesting . . ."

"I'll bring it back to Denver when the job is over," Longarm promised. "Either that, or I'll pin my own badge on him and wear yours."

"Mine says Marshal. Your badge says *Deputy* Marshal."

"So what? After I clean up Arizona, I'll deserve to be a full marshal."

Billy swore and then reached inside his coat pocket to retrieve his badge. "You lose this," he warned through the bars, "and you'd better never come back to Denver unless it's in a coffin draped with a flag."

"Aw, come on, Billy! It's just a fancy tin star."

"No," Billy said, "we both know it's a whole lot more than that."

Longarm's fingers closed around Billy's badge. "You're right, boss. And I'll either die wearing it in Arizona, or I'll bring it back to you polished and shiny."

"See that it's the latter," Billy said, reaching into his pocket for additional travel money and then adding, "and enjoy your breakfast tomorrow morning before they turn you loose from this stinking cell. There's a train heading back to Denver at seven A.M. and another heading west to Arizona two hours later, so I won't be around tomorrow to wish you the best of luck with the Grand Canyon Gang.

I'll leave a signed letter at the train station deputizing Ollie Swenson as a federal law officer."

"I'll do fine, and thanks for the extra badge. I can't tell you how much this will mean to Ollie. He's wanted to be a federal lawman since he was a boy."

"Humpf!" Billy snorted, glancing over at the snoring giant. "That just proves he's even dumber than he appears."

Longarm stifled a laugh and watched his boss quietly tiptoe back out of the office. Billy could be kind of insulting at times, but at least his heart was in the right place.

Chapter 10

Longarm and Ollie had an uneventful train ride to Flagstaff, although it was clear that those running the Santa Fe railroad became more and more worried as they approached the Arizona's Grand Canyon high country.

At a town called Holbrook just south of the Navajo Reservation, Longarm asked the conductor about the Grand Canyon Gang, and he said, "We haven't been hit by that bunch in almost two weeks."

"That's good to hear."

"No," the conductor said, looking as nervous as a long-tailed cat under a rocking chair, "it ain't. Means that this train is about to be robbed again. Last time the gang did it was on the grade up the mountain just east of Flagstaff. We were only going about five miles an hour when we rounded a bend and there was a pile of trees lying across the tracks. If we'd have been going fast on the downgrade instead of slow on the upgrade, we'd have crashed into them trees and derailed. As it was, the engineer was able to stop in time, but that's when the gang jumped us. Put a gun to the engineer's head, and when I jumped down from this coach, they got the drop on me, too! I thought they were gonna kill me."

"But they just robbed the passengers and the mail car?"

"And me!" the conductor said angrily. "Took all the money I was carrying and my watch and chain."

"That's better than taking your life."

"Sure is, but when they were done robbing and beating us, they shot the head off one of our passengers."

"Why?"

"He was a wealthy man on his way to San Francisco, and he'd been drinking. When they took all his money and jewelry, he sassed the gang and paid the price for his foolishness. You should have heard the ladies scream up in the first-class coach."

"I'll bet."

"Did you see any of the gang's faces?"

"Nope. They were all wearing masks. Most of them were big fellas like yourself but not as huge as your deputy. By golly, that fella is a giant!"

"He's that, alright," Longarm agreed. "Do you remember anything else about the gang members? Something that might help me recognize them?"

"I do recall that several of them had red hair, which made me suspect they were related to each other."

"Is that a fact?"

"Yeah, but their hair wasn't bright red so it would stand out in a crowd. Their hair was kinda reddish brown, and they had pale blue eyes set kinda close together and real deep in their faces."

"I'll remember that," Longarm told the conductor. "Were they holding pistols or rifles?"

"Both," the man said. "A couple of them had shotguns, and I knew right away that they'd unleash both barrels on anyone who gave them any lip. That's what the rich fella headed for California got . . . two loads of shot . . . one in the head and the body. The first blast blew his head almost completely off and smattered his brains all over the seat and walls. It was a terrible sight."

"They kill or hurt anyone else?"

"They violated a couple of the ladies in the first-class coach."

"What do you mean by that?"

"I mean," the conductor swore, "that they raped them in their berths."

"I see. Sounds to me like they're just a bunch of animals."

"Worse."

Longarm nodded in agreement and went back to the second-class coach and his assistant deputy. "Ollie," he said, "we've got our work cut out for us on this job."

"Is that right?"

"Yep. This could be the bloodiest bunch I've ever tried to kill or capture, and I've seen some bad ones before."

"Well," the giant said, "we didn't come here to go on a damned picnic."

Longarm looked at the man, wondering if he really understood what they would soon be up against. But Ollie had turned to stare out the window, and his face was serene and untroubled. And despite his great size, the Swede looked almost boyish and harmless, as content as a cat in a creamery.

Maybe, Longarm thought, *I made a big mistake pinning a federal officer's badge on him and agreeing to bring Ollie along on this tough assignment. Given his size and slowness, he'll make an easy target, and I'm gonna feel guilty as sin if he gets killed on my account.*

• • •

When their train finally arrived at the bustling logging and ranching town of Flagstaff, they couldn't help but be impressed by the nearby San Francisco peaks still capped with winter snow. The air was cool and crisp, the sky was indigo blue, and the town was filled with boisterous loggers, cowboys, and Navajo Indians from the nearby reservation.

Ollie took a deep breath and puffed out his barrel chest, planting his feet wide apart on the depot's worn planks. The federal marshal's badge he'd shined to a gloss was prominently on display. "Why, jimminy creepers!" he declared loud enough for everyone to hear. "This town ain't half as big or impressive as I expected. Why, it ain't even half the size of Santa Fe."

"Nope, but it's growing fast," Longarm said, picking up his bags and looking around. "I was through here six or seven years ago, and it's at least tripled in size since that time. Flagstaff appears to be prospering."

"So what do we do first?"

"We find a hotel and clean up," Longarm said, rubbing the stubble on his chin. "We haven't shaved or enjoyed baths in four days, and you smell like a goat."

Ollie looked chagrined. "I do?"

"Yep," Longarm said. "But don't let that bother you, because I'm sure I smell just as rank. I'm also hungry for a good meal."

"Now you're talkin'," Ollie agreed, a big grin spreading across his face. "We ain't been eating too regular since we left Santa Fe."

"Get used to it," Longarm warned. "Once we rent horses and get after the Grand Canyon Gang, we're probably going to start missing a lot of meals."

Ollie paled. "We will?"

"Sure," Longarm said. "What did you think a federal

marshal does when he's out in the field trying to bring down a bunch of thieves and killers? Just sit in an office like you did in Santa Fe and wait for them to surrender?"

"Well, no, but I didn't think we'd have to go without regular eats."

"Ollie, I'm thinking that you might not have thought this whole thing through very well. For starters, we don't have offices and we don't rest our feet up on a desk because we're constantly on the move."

"I guess that makes sense."

"So let's find a hotel, clean up, and find out if the town council has found a new local marshal."

"What happened to the old one?"

"He was gunned down by the Grand Canyon Gang, and the last I heard, the gang had warned the city council that they'd better not hire a replacement."

"Oh."

Longarm headed up the street with his bags, looking for a hotel. When he came upon the two-story brick Excelsior Hotel, he judged it to be one of the better establishments Flagstaff had to offer.

"We gonna share a room?" Ollie asked as they entered the lobby. " 'Cause, if we are, you better know right away that I snore pretty loud."

"I know you do," Longarm said. "I heard you plenty already."

"Well, I thought you ought to be warned."

Longarm paid for his own room and told Ollie to do the same. The giant looked hurt when he said, "I thought the federal government would pay for everything."

"We're on an unusually tight budget this trip," Longarm told the man. "Besides, you'll get compensated for what you spend. I'll keep it all in my head."

"In that case," Ollie said, looking relieved, "I don't mind payin'."

Longarm watched his assistant deputy pull out a roll of greenbacks large enough to choke a mule. Ollie must have cashed in his life savings before leaving Santa Fe. Longarm didn't ask, but it appeared the man was carrying four or five hundred dollars.

"Maybe," Longarm said, "you ought to open a bank account here."

"Now why would I want to do that?"

"In case we get in trouble," Longarm said. "People see you carrying that much money just invites thieves and pickpockets."

But Ollie shook his head. "Anyone tries to pick my pocket, and I'll break their neck like it was a chicken bone."

"You can't do that wearing a federal officer's badge."

"Why not? They'd be stealin' from me, wouldn't they?"

"Yes," Longarm said patiently, "but picking a pocket is not a capital offense."

"A what?"

Longarm noticed that the hotel desk clerk was looking alarmed by this conversation, so he said, "Ollie, I'll explain it later."

"Okay."

The desk clerk was thin, with eyes that did not stop blinking behind a pair of thick spectacles. Of medium height and in his early sixties, his skin was as dry as parchment paper and just about as colorless. "Gentlemen," he said, his voice a nasal whine, "I see that you are *federal* law officers."

"That's right," Ollie said proudly. "We come to capture or kill the Grand Canyon Gang."

"Good luck," the clerk said tolerantly. "Others have tried and paid for their effort with their lives."

"We're not 'others,' " Ollie told the man. "We're better than the ones who already tried and failed."

"Glad to hear that. I'm giving you rooms on the first floor and . . ."

Longarm interrupted the man. "I want adjoining rooms on the second floor overlooking the main street."

"Cost you a dollar a night extra."

"No it won't," Longarm said, giving the man a hard, uncompromising look. "In fact, we expect a discount because we are here to help Flagstaff and the law-abiding people who live in this part of Arizona."

The clerk's eyes dropped a moment before he said, "We don't have any law now. I suppose you know that our marshal was gunned down. And no one has been brave enough to take his place."

Longarm said, "We mean to make this town and the surrounding countryside safe again. So give us our rooms, send up hot water for baths, and let's quit the talk."

"Yes sir," the man said. "Will you be wanting anything besides rooms and baths?"

"Like what?" Longarm said.

"Like . . . well, you know."

"No, I don't."

"Marshal," the clerk said, looking frustrated. "We're not boys. I was just wondering if you would enjoy the company of *ladies*."

"I would!" Ollie said, his eyes taking on a lustful shine.

"I'll pass," Longarm said. "I'm not in the habit of paying women for their favors."

"It's a lot cheaper than marrying them," the clerk said, trying to be amusing.

"I guess it would be," Longarm said, "but I'm not interested in marriage, either."

"I'd get married, if I found one young, rich, and pretty," Ollie offered, fairly licking his thick lips.

"I thought you wanted to be a lawman," Custis said.

"I do."

Longarm shook his head. "You can't very well be both married and a lawman always on the move."

"I don't see why not," Ollie replied. "If I was to find the right woman and get hitched, maybe my wife would like it better if I was gone chasin' after outlaws most of the time."

"Hmmm," Longarm mused aloud. "I think you might have something there, Ollie."

They got their rooms and baths and then went to the barbershop for shaves and haircuts. That accomplished, Ollie stood before the mirror and shined his badge again on the cuff of his shirtsleeve.

"You keep polishing it," Longarm teased, "and you'll wear it out."

"What are we going to do now?"

"Let's go over to the marshal's office and see what we can find."

The marshal's office was locked, and it took a while to learn that the man who owned the gunsmith shop next door not only had the keys to the office but was the town's mayor. His name was Ed Wilson, and he did not seem all that happy to have federal marshals in his company.

"So you boys are the big, bad federal marshals who have come to save Flagstaff from the Grand Canyon Gang, huh?"

Longarm had already decided he did not particularly like this man, and now Wilson was probably being sarcastic, which made him even more unlikable. "We've come to put a halt to the lawlessness in this part of Arizona."

"Well," the mayor and gunsmith drawled, sizing both Ollie and Custis up and down, "you fellas are sure big enough to handle yourselves, but your size will make you easy targets for ambushers."

"We don't expect to make ourselves 'easy targets' for anyone," Longarm snapped back with irritation. "But we would like to make use of the marshal's office while we are in town."

"What for?" Wilson asked with unexpected bluntness.

"It's helpful to have a place to keep our stuff, and I'd expect to find some handcuffs and maybe some rifles in there that would prove useful."

"Everything in the office belongs to the City of Flagstaff."

Longarm had had about enough of this man. "Listen to me, mayor. We've come a long way to try to straighten out the trouble in northern Arizona. It's my understanding that your bank has been robbed; your citizens have been killed, beaten, and raped; and the Santa Fe Railroad is about to cut off service because it's been hit so many times that it can't continue to stand the losses. Isn't that all true?"

"It's true, alright." Wilson sighed. "If the Santa Fe Railroad even cuts back on the number of its runs through our town, it'll create quite a hardship. We not only ship a lot of cattle but also timber. And the railroad has a roundhouse and shops here so our merchants enjoy quite a few of its payroll dollars."

"Then why are you being so short-sighted about loaning us the use of this office?"

"I'm just looking to protect the city's investment."

"Hogwash! Listen to me, Mayor. If you want to be difficult and uncooperative, we could go on to the next town and set up shop. Would that make you and your citizens happier?"

"No, Marshal, it would not," Wilson was forced to nervously admit as he reached into his coat pocket. "Here's the key to the office. But as the mayor of this town, I will hold you responsible to return any weapons or things that you take in the commission of your duty."

"We ain't the ones who are thieves," Ollie snorted with derision. "And you ought not to talk to a federal officer of the law in such a mean-spirited manner."

Wilson started to snap back a reply, but when Ollie advanced a step and towered over the mayor, he had a sudden change of mind.

After the mayor went back into his own shop, Longarm used the key to open the vacated town marshal's office. It was about what he'd expected and what he'd seen many times in these small frontier towns. There were two battered desks with chairs, a pair of small jail cells in the back, and a potbellied stove on the east wall.

"Look," Ollie said, moving past the desks to the gun rack, which he opened for display. "There are rifles in here and also a sawed-off shotgun. Twelve gauge—and it's a beauty."

Longarm nodded with satisfaction. "There are also two cots over there with woolen blankets. I think maybe we ought to move into this office in order to save our travel money as much as possible."

"You want us to sleep in here?"

"We won't be hanging around that much," Longarm told the giant. "But every dollar we save on a room we can put to good use."

"Like on women and beer?"

Longarm frowned. "Ollie, I don't care what you do with your own time, because you're all grown up now. But I won't ever tolerate you getting drunk while we're working together. It's not only unbecoming a federal officer, it's outright dangerous. Never forget that there are always men who hate anyone wearing a tin star. And sometimes, they hate us with good reason, as every lawman is not just. But even more important and to the point, those same men will kill us if they catch us drunk or off our guard. Do you understand me?"

"Yes sir!"

"Good. And remember, now that we're here in Arizona, people are going to know why we came and what we hope to accomplish. Federal marshals aren't sent to a town so they can have a good time and become everyone's friend."

"I know that."

"Then know that we will be marked for bullets. I've no doubt that this gang moves freely in these railroad towns because they always wear masks when they strike. That being the case, it's impossible to know who is a friend and who is a deadly enemy."

Ollie nodded with understanding. "I'm just beginning to realize that being a federal officer in a strange town is a whole lot different than being a local marshal or deputy."

"I'm glad you appreciate the difference," Longarm told the big man.

"What are we going to do now?" Ollie asked.

"Lock up and go find a good steak."

"Now you're talkin'! And maybe later, I'll have a private little chat with that desk clerk and find out what a pretty woman costs here in Flagstaff."

"Suit yourself," Longarm told him as they headed outside. "Just don't let her steal all your money."

107

"You mean like Emerald stole *your* money?"

Longarm didn't bother with an answer as he headed back outside. They didn't walk fifty feet when they smelled fresh-cooked apple pie. Longarm peered through the window of a café and saw that it was busy but that there were a few empty tables.

"How about this place?" he asked.

"Smells great," Ollie replied, already reaching for the door handle.

When they walked inside and sat down, Longarm noticed a sign that read: WELCOME TO BIG ANNIE AND LITTLE LILLY'S PLACE! EXPECT *GOOD* FOOD IN EXCHANGE FOR *GOOD* MANNERS.

"See that sign over the counter?" Longarm asked his assistant deputy.

Ollie looked at it blankly. "What's it say?"

"You can't read?"

"No."

Longarm read the sign for him and then added, "It means that you don't eat like a starved hog, Ollie. You cut your food up with a knife and feed it into your mouth with a fork and you wipe your lips with a napkin. You don't belch, and you don't fart."

"Sure are a lot of rules just to eat by," Ollie said absently. "I just hope they feed us fast."

Longarm was about to say something when he changed his mind and stared. "Holy smokes! Wait until you get an eyeful of what's coming to our table."

Ollie twisted around, and his eyes widened as the blonde and buxom waitress smiled. She stood well over six feet tall and had big blue eyes. She wasn't beautiful, but she was pleasant looking and in her mid-thirties. Longarm estimated that she weighed about two hundred fifty pounds and that most of it was muscle.

"Hi big boy!" she said, looking only at Ollie. "Why, I'll bet you can eat half a steer all by your lonesome."

"I sure could! You sound Swedish."

"I sure am. Annie Olsen is my name." She stuck out her hand. "What's yours?"

"Ollie Swenson." He smiled and engulfed her hand. "I'm a federal marshal."

"So I can see," Annie told him. "And a handsome one, too."

Ollie damned near split his face grinning.

"What will you have to eat, big boy? Our specialty is a two-pound steak on top of a pound of mashed potatoes."

"That sounds good, and for dessert, I'd like an apple pie."

"The whole pie?" Annie asked with her pale, upraised eyebrows.

"Yes ma'am!"

"You got it, big boy."

Longarm watched with amusement, and when the two Swedes finally got around to realizing he was sitting at the table, he also ordered the two-pound steak but decided to wait and see if he had enough stomach for apple pie.

"Ain't she a beautiful woman!" Ollie whispered when the café's part-owner was gone.

"She is that."

"And Swedish, too!" Ollie slapped the table with his huge paw so hard the salt and pepper shakers and their silverware jumped at least a foot. "My oh my. This could be my lucky day!"

But Longarm wasn't really listening, because another woman, probably Annie's partner, Lilly, had appeared. She wasn't actually little, unless you compared her to Big Annie. She was maybe five feet four and a hundred twenty pounds, but every bit of it was arranged right.

She was a brunette, and as she poured coffee and served the other tables, Longarm couldn't help but find her very attractive. When she sneaked a glance at him, he gave her his best and most friendly smile. He was rewarded with a smile in return and then a wink.

Maybe, he thought, *it's both Ollie's and my lucky day.*

Chapter 11

As they left the café, Longarm turned and made a mental note that it closed at eight P.M. every evening. "Maybe," he said to Ollie, "we ought to come by around that time and see if Annie and Lilly need some protection on their way home. Flagstaff is a pretty rough town, and two pretty women like that need special attention."

"Now you're talkin'!" Ollie said, rubbing his stomach. "That was one of the best dinners I ever ate."

"I've never seen anyone put away so much food," Longarm told the man. "I couldn't believe you finished that whole apple pie on top of the monster steak and all those potatoes."

Ollie belched. "I normally wouldn't have eaten that much, but I wanted to impress Big Annie. Swedes know how to pack the food away because our ancestors didn't eat all the time and it was always cold where they lived. A Swede has to learn to eat like a horse 'cause he might not get to eat again for days."

To prove his point, Ollie belched and then farted so loud it made heads turn on the street.

"We've got some time to kill," Longarm told his ill-mannered assistant. "Let's make good use of it."

Ollie stretched and then yawned. "I was thinking of taking a little nap to let my food settle. It's not real healthy to do much after having a big meal."

"We need to start our investigation now," Longarm said, ignoring Ollie's objection. "I'll start down the other side of the street asking questions about the Grand Canyon Gang. You cover this side."

"Who do I ask and what do I say?"

"I want you to talk to everyone—people standing on the boardwalk, people in the shops and saloons. Tell them who you are and why we're here. Let it be known that we are after the gang and won't quit until we see them either dead . . . or behind prison bars."

"Won't that stir things up and give the gang a warning?"

"Sure," Longarm said, "given enough time. But it also might get us some leads so we can strike before the gang knows we're here to bring them down. It's a gamble, but I'm not the kind of man to sit around and wait for things to happen. It's better to make them happen and then see where the chips fall."

"Alright," Ollie said, hitching up his gun and starting to turn away so he could start questioning everyone he saw.

"One thing you need to keep in mind, Ollie."

The giant swiveled around on his boot heels. "Yeah?"

"Try to get people alone when you talk to them. Also, do a whole lot more listening than yappin'. If you can get any descriptions or names, be sure to write them down."

"I can't read nor write," Ollie reminded Longarm. "But I got a good memory for faces. If anyone knows anyone in the Grand Canyon Gang, I'll pry it out of them . . . one way or another."

"No rough stuff!" Longarm warned. "You're a federal officer of the law now, and we don't go around acting like we're the law unto ourselves."

"What does that mean?"

"Just keep your hands off people and don't threaten to break their bones," Longarm explained. "Be polite to the ladies, even the old and cantankerous ones, and be professional with all the men you meet. If you try to intimidate or press them too hard, they'll work against us out of spite."

"I understand," Ollie said, one big hand absently caressing his shiny badge. "And you don't have to worry about me hurtin' anyone unless they try to hurt me first."

"That's the attitude I want to hear."

Longarm left his man and headed across the street. He wasn't really expecting to learn much from the townspeople, although he'd probably hear a lot of wild conjecture that had no basis in fact. Either way, they had to try.

"Excuse me," Longarm said to a clerk sweeping the boardwalk in front of his store. "My name is Marshal Custis Long, and I'd like to ask you a few questions."

"About what?" the clerk asked suspiciously.

"About the death of your town marshal and the bunch that is terrorizing this part of Arizona."

The clerk was a skinny fella in his thirties with buck teeth, close-set eyes, and sunken cheeks. In response to Longarm's request, he started sweeping faster. "I don't know much about any of that," he said, facing into the rising cloud of dust. "You oughta ask someone else. I just try to mind my own business and get along with everyone."

"You aren't getting along with me very well right now," Longarm said, placing a hand on the broom. "How did your town marshal die?"

"He was shot down during a bank holdup," the clerk said, looking around nervously. "But I didn't see it happen. Lots of others did, though. I can't tell you nothin', Marshal, and I need to get this walk swept clean."

Longarm was disgusted. "Yeah, I guess you couldn't at that. Do you own this little butcher shop?"

"No sir. I just work for the man who does."

"That figures."

Longarm left the clerk, and the next man he approached was a lean cowboy who was sitting propped back on a three-legged chair in front of a saddle shop. The cowboy looked tired and discouraged. He had a bandage covering one side of his face, and his arm was splinted and resting in a dirty bandanna serving as a sling.

"Busted arm?" Longarm asked.

"Busted as a stick. Doc tried to set the bones, but I'd waited too long to ride from my line shack in and he says my left arm will always look like it has two elbows instead of just one. Says I won't never have much strength in it again, and it'll give me pain for the rest of my natural life."

"Horse throw you?"

"Nope. I was trying to fetch a mountain goat I'd shot on the rim of the Grand Canyon. Goat fell over the side and landed on a ledge about fifty feet down off the rim. I tied one end of my rope to my saddle horn and the other around my chest then eased on down the side until I reached the dyin' goat. I was doin' my damndest to bring the goat back up on top of the rim when my horse got bit by a rattlesnake and ran off."

"Sounds like you were in a real bad wreck."

"It was even worse than it sounds. The goat still had some life, and before I knew it, he hooked me in the eye with his horn. That horn plucked my eyeball out as clean as you'd suck the seed from a ripe plum."

Longarm shook his head with genuine sympathy. "So what are you going to do now?"

"Probably starve or die of self-pity if I don't find some way to make money. Boss over at the Bar Six fired me on the spot for being so stupid as to get myself in such a bad fix. My horse ran until it dropped and died of snake poison."

Longarm didn't quite know what to say to the tragic cowboy. "We all go through some rough skids in life."

"That we do," the cowboy agreed, managing a smile that showed he was missing most of his upper front teeth. "I hear that you and that overgrown ape who came in on the train are *federal* marshals."

"That's right. We're here to catch the Grand Canyon Gang."

"You might when hell freezes over."

Longarm frowned. "Now why would you say that?"

" 'Cause you're strangers to these parts. Do you have any idea how big this country is? And how rugged?"

"Everyplace is big west of the Rockies. I've chased killers and thieves all over Texas, Montana, New Mexico, Wyoming, and plenty of other places. Big doesn't scare me even a little bit."

"Glad to hear that. Big spaces never scared me, neither." The cowboy eased his chair down on its three legs and then unfolded and came to his feet. He was as tall as Longarm but probably weighed about half as much. He was as brown as an old boot with skin cracked and dry from too many years in the saddle.

"Marshal," he drawled, "I am desperate for a job that

don't include a broom, mop, or dishrag. I ain't willin' to string barbed wire, and with my bum arm, I ain't strong enough to cut timber or lay railroad ties. Folks tell me I'm so skinny I can't even throw a shadow."

Longarm reached into his pocket and found some money, enough for three or four meals. "Here," he said. "Feed yourself."

But the cowboy waved off the offer and looked past Longarm toward the mountains. "I ain't never taken a handout, Marshal. Never will, either. What money I get . . . I earn."

"Alright, then, tell me how I can track down and catch the men who killed Flagstaff's marshal and who rob trains, stagecoaches, and even the Navajo of their sheep."

"If I told you, it might hasten the end of your days."

"I'll take that chance."

The cowboy nodded. "You ain't got no chance here, and both you and your friend sure make big targets."

"Keep talking."

The cowboy hitched up his belt and pulled down his hat brim until it was low over his one good eye. "You need someone who can show you the places outlaws use to hide in this country. And you need someone who is friendly with the Navajo Indians, is trusted by them, and speaks a little of their language. Otherwise, you and that ape of yours won't get so much as a headstone for your graves."

"And where would I find such a man?"

"I can recommend one . . . he's me."

Longarm clucked his tongue. "A one-eyed, broken-armed ex-cowboy?"

"Why not? You're going to need to buy some horses, ain't ya? Saddles and gear, too?"

"Yes."

"I know where to find the best horses at the best prices and all the gear and outfit we'll need to head out to the rim country. And I know the trails and where you'll have to find waterholes in order to survive. This country is high and mostly dry, Marshal."

"I don't have money for a second assistant," Longarm said frankly. "The federal government gave me barely enough to outfit myself and Deputy Ollie Swenson."

"Being sort of bunged up, I'm gonna have to work real, real cheap. But if we find some of the gang's stolen money hidden under a rock or the roots of a piñon pine, there ought to be a sizable reward, wouldn't you agree?"

"I would," Longarm said.

"And I'd be in line to get a share, wouldn't I?"

"You would be," Longarm agreed. "As federal officers of the law, we can't take rewards."

"I wouldn't wear no badge or take no oath."

"Do you really know where some of the stolen money would be found?"

The cowboy smiled. "Since losin' one eye, bustin' my arm, and havin' nothing to do but listen, I've heard things. Might be I could help you recover some cash and other jewelry and stuff that's been taken."

"If that's true, I might be inclined to suspect you had something to do with the thefts."

"Nope," the cowboy said, not the least bit offended by the suggestion. "But I do know most everything that happens in this country. I could borrow a horse, and I still have a bedroll, saddle, six-shooter, and rifle. All you'd have to do is come up with my feed and a little whiskey now and then. Not much to ask considering how far you came and how little chance you and the ape have of staying alive . . . much less finding the gang and collecting the stolen loot."

"What's your name?" Longarm asked.

"Slim Wakefield."

"Can you shoot a gun and rifle?"

" 'Course I can."

"Can you hit what you aim at?"

"I still got one good eye and one good arm. I ought to be able to make the adjustment."

"If you ride with us, you'll be risking your life."

"Ain't much left to risk, is there, Marshal? I'd rather die doin' somethin' exciting than standin' around here until someone hands me a tin cup for folks to throw coins into as they're passin'."

Longarm shoved the money into Slim's faded jeans. "Go get something to eat, Slim."

"You're takin' a big chance by not hirin' me."

"How's that?"

Slim winked with his one eye. "Well, Marshal," he drawled, "some beautiful young lady might come along and find me so handsome and irresistible that she'll take me home and beg me to marry her. And when I said yes, my offer to you wouldn't stand."

Longarm had to chuckle. Slim was the saddest, most pitiful specimen of manhood imaginable, but at least the man still had a sense of humor, and that showed he had some character. Trouble was, he wouldn't last long as a lawman.

Longarm covered one side of Flagstaff talking to everyone he met. Some people acted scared half to death, like the clerk sweeping off the walk in front of the butcher shop. Others either acted as if they didn't know anything or didn't care to talk about what they did know. One old Navajo told Longarm that he wanted to take the scalps of those who were stealing his people's sheep.

Now and then, Longarm caught sight of Ollie working

the opposite side of the street. They'd exchange waves and then continue interviewing people.

As Longarm was exiting the Red Garter Saloon, a woman wearing a dark blue velvet dress called out to him. "Marshal!"

Longarm turned to see a woman who was about his own age with black hair and eyes coming over to him at the door. "Ma'am?"

"I understand you've been in here asking my bartenders and customers some tough questions."

"I'm just trying to learn what I can about the trouble you've been having with the Grand Canyon Gang. I didn't mean to upset anyone, but we have to start investigating somewhere."

"So you do it in my *saloon?*"

Longarm couldn't judge whether she was angry or not, so he said, "I don't come on strong, ma'am. I just quietly ask if anyone knows anything that might help me."

She put her hands on her hips and stared deeply into his eyes. "Don't you know that all you'll get from men who are drinking is a line of pure bullshit?"

"No," he answered, "I don't. In fact, I've been a law-man long enough to realize that a few drinks often loosens the tongue and gets me important information that I'd never have gotten from a completely sober interview."

"Hmm," she said, a slight smile lifting the corners of her lips. "I wish I could say the same. As far as I can tell, men lie when they're sober and they lie even worse when they're drunk."

"All men?"

"Yes. When I was seventeen I even knew a hellfire-and-brimstone-spoutin' preacher who could quote verse and line from the Holy Bible. He was one of the slickest little liars I ever came across. Told me he'd save my soul and give me eternal salvation, but all I got was his hard little pronger every time he got me on my back. After a while, I finally realized he wasn't interested in anything but my hot young body."

Longarm felt his cheeks warming. "I know that even some men of the cloth will yield to the flesh, ma'am. They're still only men . . . the same as the rest of us."

"And liars."

"Well," Longarm said, not seeing any more use in being insulted. "I guess I'll go on my way. Sorry if I upset any of your customers or help."

"Hold on!" she said. "My name is *Miss* Victoria, and I own this place free and clear."

"You seem to be doing well. Lots of customers."

"It'll be five deep at the bar tonight. I have a good piano man and a couple girls who can sing and dance instead of just spread their legs and collect a man's money and seed."

"You're a frank-talking woman, Miss Victoria."

"Life is too short to chew the fat all day. What did you find out from your questioning of my customers?"

"Not much, I'm afraid."

"That's because everyone is afraid someone will overhear them talking about the gang and they'll get a lead pill in their gut because of their loose lip."

Longarm nodded. "I kind of had that impression."

"So you were asking the wrong people."

"And who is the *right* person to ask?"

Victoria pursed her lips and slowly looked him up and down. "You're a big one, aren't you, Marshal?"

"Custis. I'm six foot four, if it matters."

"It might. Why don't you come around in about an hour. Only don't come in the front door. Come around to the alley and up the back steps to my office, where I might be able to help you."

"Why would you do that?"

"I have my reasons."

"I like to know who I'm dealing with and their real motivation."

Victoria shook her head and reached up to pat Longarm's cheek. "Let's just say I had two girls coming out to work for me on the train from the East when it was robbed by that gang. After them mean sons of bitches finished with my girls, they wouldn't work on their backs for anyone again. They got raped and beaten and . . . well, they weren't nuns, but they sure didn't deserve what they got from the Grand Canyon Gang. So that's my reason for maybe talking to you."

"Fair enough reason," Longarm said. "I'll be back in an hour."

"Don't make me wait."

"I won't."

An hour later, Longarm was climbing the back steps leading up to Victoria's office above her Red Garter Saloon. The piano man had arrived, and from the sound of the music and laughter, Longarm figured that the saloon was already starting to get busy. Miss Victoria had a prosperous business, and Longarm figured she must be one of the richest women in town.

"Come on in!"

Longarm entered the door, and the woman was sitting at a huge roll-top desk wearing a pink silk nightgown trimmed with black lace. The nightgown left little to the imagination, and although the saloon owner was no spring chicken, she was still luscious enough for any healthy man to want to feast upon.

"Have a drink, Marshal Custis."

"Marshal Long. But just call me Custis. I'll have whiskey."

"Good choice. I import my best from Boston. I think you'll approve."

She poured them both glasses, bending over slightly so he could see all the way down her pink nightgown. Victoria pretended not to notice him taking his visual liberties, and when she straightened and handed Longarm his glass she said, "To the death of the Grand Canyon Gang."

"To bringing them to a hangman's rope and true justice," he amended.

Their eyes locked and she said, "And to your health, Custis. You're going to need to be both very good and very lucky."

They drank and then Victoria said, "There's another reason why I want to bring that gang to justice, and I might as well tell you now because you'll hear about it soon enough."

"What's that?"

"I was in love with the marshal they gunned down during their last bank holdup. Abner was one of the finest men I ever met. He ran out in the street trying to protect a child from being run over in the gunfire and confusion, and when he reached for her, they shot him down like a dog."

Longarm could see a shine and intense pain in her eyes now. "I'm sorry."

"Not as sorry as I am," Victoria said. "The funny thing is that Abner was the *second* lawman I've fallen in love with."

"Is that a fact?" he said, not at all sure where this was leading.

"It is," Victoria told him as she placed her drink down

and reached around his waist. "And as tall and handsome as you are, Custis, watch out or you might become lawman number three."

He gulped down his drink and breathed in her perfume. She was a handsome woman, and she smelled like springtime lilacs. "I thought you asked me up here to tell me about the Grand Canyon Gang."

"I did, but that wasn't the main reason."

He still didn't completely trust her. She was too smooth and confident. "There are a lot of tall men in this town. Some a lot better looking than me."

"Let's just say that a man who lives dangerously strikes my fancy. Also, before I met Abner, I'd already enjoyed all the handsome ones in Flagstaff who have any spirit. Have you got spirit, Custis?"

"I might."

Victoria unbuckled his belt and then his trousers. She reached inside and found his flaccid manhood that was quickly turning hard. "Why don't we find out exactly how much spirit and sap you have inside."

Longarm knew he wasn't being very professional, but his body was also telling him that he was a man in need of some passionate loving. So what the hell. He wasn't sure of Victoria's real game, but it looked as if he was going to make love to her before he'd have any chance of finding it out. He unbuckled his gun belt and removed his coat, vest, and watch.

"Over here on the couch," she whispered, taking his stiff rod in both hands before leading him over to the couch as if he were a young stallion. "It'll fit us just fine."

Longarm tore off his shirt while Victoria untied a bow at her throat and showed him everything she had to offer. He gulped, felt his manhood throb and stretch, then he eased her down on the couch and kissed her lips, her throat, and her lovely breasts.

"Oh my," she said, "keep going in my southerly direction."

Victoria smelled so clean and good that he would have gone down farther even if she hadn't asked. And when he was where she really wanted him to be, she began to cry out with pleasure so loud and free that he feared she might be heard over the music down in the saloon.

"Oh, Custis," she moaned as he pressed her thighs apart and had a dessert that was better than any homemade apple pie. "You are so good to me!"

He came up for a breath of air. "About as good as you're going to be to me in a few minutes."

Longarm stayed down on her until Victoria grew so frantic that her powerful thighs were cutting off his air supply. Both of them now gasping, he raised up and looked into her eyes glazed with bright pleasure.

"My turn," she panted, pushing him back and attacking him as if she were a starving beast. Longarm spread his own thighs and watched as she worked him over until he couldn't keep his hips from jerking. "Enough," he finally groaned.

"Not enough," she argued, sucking even harder.

But Longarm wanted the thing that pleased him most, and that was to bury his big tool deep into her hot wetness and fill her with his fiery seed. When he entered Victoria, she was wet and ready, and she immediately locked her legs around his waist and began pumping.

"Slow down," he urged. "We aren't in a race. Let's make it last."

"Isn't that supposed to be *my* line?"

Longarm chuckled and cupped her lovely bottom in his hand, then went even deeper into her juicy womanhood.

He moved slow and steady until Victoria was clawing at his back and screaming loud enough to be heard not only in the Red Garter, but in every other saloon in Flagstaff.

"Now!" he bellowed as they both lost complete control and entered into their sweet, mindless madness.

She bit him on the neck and raked his back with her nails. Victoria's shapely legs went up in the air as she bucked and screamed until she was hoarse and then suddenly went limp.

Longarm knew he wanted a full night with this wildcat saloon owner. He finally eased himself off her and nearly toppled to the floor. Righting himself, he sagged into a chair and reached for the whiskey to refill their glasses.

"You gonna fall in love with lawman number three?" he asked with a grin.

"Already have, Custis. But don't you go and get killed by the gang before I've had my complete fill of you . . . which could take about twenty years."

Handing Victoria her glass, he pulled her close and said, "Do you really have something I can use?"

"Honey," she breathed, shaking her beautiful breasts and then pushing them out to show him that her nipples were as hard as rubies, "it felt like you could use these real well."

"You know what I meant."

"Oh, yes. You want me to help you catch and kill the Grand Canyon Gang."

"Capture them if I can. Kill them if I must."

Victoria kissed his mouth with surprising tenderness. "You know something? I'm really tempted to tell you nothing so you don't get hurt or worse."

"I'm a big boy with an even bigger deputy to help."

"I've heard about him. One of my girls says he's as big as a hillside."

"Not quite. Ollie Swenson is attracted to Big Annie over at the café. Is there any hope for that?"

"Sure is," she told him. "Annie is a good woman. Swedish, and she's been looking for a husband for quite some time."

"Was she married before?"

"Yes," Victoria said. "Word is that she screwed her husband into an early grave. He had a heart attack one night, and when the doctor rushed to his bedside, there was evidence that he died a very happy and satisfied man. I heard a well-known rumor that the undertaker had one hell of a time getting the grin off his poor dead face."

Longarm had to chuckle. "Well," he said, "Ollie isn't the quickest man either on the draw or uptake. But he's got a good heart, and he is quite smitten with that big blonde."

"Then they might be a match made in Swedish heaven," Victoria said. "So were you giving Lilly the eye?"

"I couldn't help but notice her," Longarm admitted as he stroked Victoria's silky thighs. "But now I've got you on my mind . . . along with the gang."

"The gang," she said, brow furrowing as she touched the rim of her glass to his. "What I have to say might take a while with some serious interruptions for wild sexual pleasuring."

"I've got no plans for the night."

"Good," Victoria said, rubbing the hair on his chest. "Then I'll tell you what I know about the Grand Canyon Gang and how much I want them all dead."

A short while ago, Longarm had wondered if Victoria might be setting him up for a trap. But now, as he listened to the bitterness in her voice and remembered how the

Grand Canyon Gang had shot down the lawman she'd loved and violated the two women on the train, he knew that whatever this woman told him would be the whole and unvarnished truth.

Chapter 12

"So," Longarm asked as they reclined naked on Victoria's couch, "let's talk about the Grand Canyon Gang."

She raised an eyebrow. "Custis, you are a *serious* man."

"I've come a long way to take care of some bad business. And I know you want to see that bunch captured or killed as much as anyone in northern Arizona."

"I do," she said, her face set with resolve. "Abner and those girls I sent for from Boston didn't deserve what they got, and there are a lot of other people being hurt by the gang—including the Navajo, who have very little to lose."

"Do you know who they are?"

Victoria's lips drew into a thin line. "I don't know for sure, but I have my suspicions. There are several men who come into my saloon at least once a week, and I can't help but think they are part of the gang."

"Describe them for me."

"The ones I'm thinking of look as if they are related. They're big men, like you, but not nearly so handsome."

"What color hair do they have?" Longarm asked.

"They have reddish-brown hair. More red than brown."

129

"Have they ever spoken about the Grand Canyon Gang?"

"No. They come in, buy a bottle or two, and take a table away from most of my other customers. Once or twice they've played faro or poker, but usually they just sit and get drunk. They're not rowdy, but they don't have to be."

"What does that mean?"

"It means that they give the impression of being very tough hombres. No one in their right or sober mind would go over and try to strike up a conversation with this bunch I'm describing."

"I understand. Do they come in any particular night?"

"Let's see," Victoria mused aloud. "Yes, as a matter of fact. They do seem to come in on Saturday or Sunday night."

"Perhaps they have regular jobs."

"Maybe," she said.

"Are they armed?"

"To the teeth."

"Do they get drunk?"

Victoria shrugged. "Yeah, I guess they do. Like I said, they don't get loud or rowdy, but they drink plenty. Why is that important?"

Longarm didn't answer. "What time do they generally arrive at your Red Garter?"

"Early evening."

"And when do they leave?"

"After midnight."

"Do they look like railroad men, cowboys, or lumbermen?"

Victoria thought a moment. "They're not cowboys. They might be lumbermen, but I have the feeling they work for the railroad. Say, you sure are asking a lot of questions."

"They're important," Longarm assured her. "If me and my assistant just brace the men, they'll either fight or throw up their hands and deny they're part of any gang. So what I'd like to do is wait until they get drunk and careless, then follow them to wherever they take me."

"I see. That way, you can see if there are more of them."

"That, or maybe I'll go back to their place on Monday when they return to work and search wherever it is they live."

"Makes sense," Victoria said, looking impressed. "And the other good thing is that today is Friday so you don't have to wait long."

"That's right."

"But I have to tell you that these redheads don't come in every weekend. Sometimes, they disappear for several weeks at a time."

"And what does that suggest?"

"That they're holding up a stage or staging a raid on someone or some place?"

"Exactly!"

Victoria was getting excited. "Is there something I can do to help you?"

"Not really. Is there anyone else who strikes you as suspicious?"

"As a matter of fact, I've been confused about our town banker."

"Meaning?"

"Well," Victoria said, "our bank has been hit twice, and both times it lost a lot of money. The gang just seemed to know what days there would be big deposits from the local timber mills and the railroad workers."

Longarm frowned. "That's easy information to get. All anyone would have to do would be to watch the bank and see when most laborers' people are making payroll deposits."

"I suppose you're right," Victoria said. "But the strange thing is that our banker, Mr. Walker, just happened to be out on errands each time our bank was robbed."

"Probably just a coincidence," Longarm said.

"And was it a coincidence that the gang knew the bank vault's combination during *both* robberies?"

"They knew that?" Longarm asked in amazement.

"That's the inside information I've heard. The vault number has been changed a third time, but the locksmith doesn't believe it will help."

"Maybe *he's* the insider, not the banker."

"Could be," Victoria answered. "But I'm betting Mr. Walker is the real culprit. Custis, are you aware that vaults in Prescott, Williams, Seligman, and even the ones on the Santa Fe Railroad have been cracked?"

"I didn't know that."

"It's possible that all the people in charge of those vaults are working with the Grand Canyon Gang, but that seems improbable to me."

"I guess it does at that. And the more I think of it, the more . . ."

There was a sharp rapping on the door, and Victoria yelled, "Who is it?"

"It's Garth, Miss Victoria," the voice called. "Don't mean to disturb you, but if that tall federal marshal is in there with you, he might like to know that his friend the badge-totin' giant is in one hell of a fight over at the Tall Pine Saloon. They've got him down and are beatin' the hell out of him right now."

Longarm jumped up and pulled on his pants and boots

and then strapped on his gun belt. He grabbed his shirt on the way out the door and heard Victoria yell something at him from the upper floor landing, but he didn't hear what she said.

"Where's the Tall Pine Saloon?" he shouted at a man.

"Just across the street and up a block!"

Longarm burst into the street, running hard. He dodged through the wagon and horse traffic and knocked two men spinning as he ran headlong down the boardwalk. Two bloodied men were standing in front of the Tall Pine looking dazed and battered, but Longarm could hear a fight going on inside the saloon. He burst through the batwing doors and skidded to a halt. Five men had Ollie Swenson backed up in a corner. Ollie towered head and shoulders over all of them, but he was so bloody that his face was scarcely recognizable.

Longarm drew his six-gun and shouted. "Hold it!"

When the five men didn't pay him any mind, Longarm fired his gun twice into the ceiling, and that got their attention. As they turned around, Ollie hammered two of them to the side of their heads, knocking them both halfway across the sawdust-covered floor. The other three jumped back, and before Longarm could act, Ollie threw his huge arms out like a bear and tackled them all to the floor.

"Stop!" Longarm shouted.

But the fight was still on as Ollie and the three men kicked, gouged, and punched in a rolling mass of blood and flesh. They didn't quit until Longarm fired another round into the ceiling and then pistol-whipped two of the fighters and let Ollie finish the last man.

"What the hell is going on here?" Longarm demanded.

"We got into a fight."

"I can see that. Why?"

Ollie crawled to his feet. He was a mess, and the men he'd been fighting looked even worse. "They insulted me and my badge. Then, they called Big Annie a *cow* and said her udders were as big as beer kegs," Ollie said, looking down at the shirt he was wearing, which had been torn to shreds. "My badge!" he cried. "It's gone!"

"We'll find it," Longarm promised, because it was really his own badge. "Don't worry. We'll find it."

Longarm dragged the three brawlers to their feet and shoved them up against a wall. He made sure they were unarmed and then turned them around, his gun still in his fist but now pointed at their battered faces. "Do you men know what happens when you assault an officer of the law?"

One of them, with his lips as red as mashed cherries, rasped, "That big son of a bitch attacked us!"

"All five of you?"

"That's right. We were sitting at a table payin' poker and minding our own business. And besides, we didn't call Annie a cow, we said she reminded us of a big draft mare."

"And they said she was stupid!" Ollie hissed, his hands still clenched.

"Well, she *is* stupid," one of the men said, wiping blood from his nose.

Ollie lashed out and hit the man, who bounced off the wall, howling. Fresh blood poured from his nose. Ollie would have gone after the last pair standing and beaten them senseless if Longarm hadn't blocked the enraged deputy's path.

"That's enough!" Longarm yelled. "Ollie, stop it or you're no longer my assistant federal marshal!"

Ollie looked confused. "You'd do that even though it

was them five who started the fight by insulting me and then Big Annie?"

"A federal officer isn't supposed to attack someone for being insulting."

"Humpf!" Ollie snorted, obviously thinking this was not only unfair, but ridiculous as well. "That ain't the way it was in Santa Fe."

"This isn't Santa Fe. And you're no longer a local officer of the law. Do we understand each other?" Longarm knew he was coming down hard on the big Swede, but there was no alternative. Ollie had to learn to control his temper. As big as the man was, he was going to kill someone or else get shot or stabbed to death.

"Yes, sir."

Satisfied, Longarm turned to the men and said, "Pick up your friends and get out of here. And if you get insulting again, I'll toss every damned one of you in the town jail and throw away the key."

Those left standing managed to drag their fallen friends out the door.

Longarm looked at Ollie and shook his head with disgust. "Deputy Marshal Swenson, we've got some talking to do. Clean yourself up, then meet me at the marshal's office."

"Can't I look for my badge first?"

"Alright," Longarm said, knowing that the badge was important to both of them for pretty much the same reasons.

In a few minutes, half the customers at the Tall Pine were down on their hands and knees sifting through the filthiest sawdust imaginable. It took about ten minutes, but the badge was found. Although it had obviously been stomped on a few times, Ollie was able to bend it back into its former shape.

"See," he said, offering a happy but bloody grin as he fixed it back on what was left of his shirt, "it's as good as new."

"Sure," Longarm said, deciding to go back to Victoria's to collect his vest, hat, and coat. "I'll see you later at the office."

"Yes, sir!"

When they exited the saloon, they heard a shout, and Big Annie came running up to them. "Ollie!" she cried, grabbing his big moon face with both hands. "What did those men do to you?"

"Aw," he drawled, "we just had a misunderstanding."

"I heard that you fought for my honor."

Ollie's face was swollen, bloody, and battered, but the giant could still blush. "I just don't like anyone talking bad about a pretty lady such as yourself."

"That's so sweet," Big Annie purred as she took his battered hands. "You come on over to my place, and I'll fix you up as good as new."

Ollie cracked a wide smile, and when he turned to leave, he winked at Longarm, who decided Ollie might not be quite as dumb as he appeared.

Longarm thought about going back to see Victoria, but he decided he ought to head for the office and decide exactly what he was going to say to Ollie. One thing was for sure—if he didn't put a tighter rein on his big assistant deputy, Ollie wasn't going to last very long.

He took three steps and didn't hear the rifle shot that boomed across the street and shattered a storefront window just inches in front of his face. Longarm instinctively knew that the ambusher was going to fire again and dove through the nearest open doorway as a second bullet struck a pickle barrel and created a stream of sweet-smelling pickle juice that drenched the legs of his pants.

Drawing his gun and trying to scoot free of the stinking juice, he turned and surveyed the street, then the windows of every building where an ambusher could hide and take good aim.

People on the street were still diving for cover; a well-dressed man and woman in a surrey went flying off toward the railroad depot, and a woman with a baby in her arms stood paralyzed in front of a dress shop. Her face was as white as a bridal dress in the storefront window.

"Get back inside!" Longarm shouted.

But the woman was struck dumb with terror. Finally, someone did pull her inside the dress shop.

Longarm searched hard, but he still couldn't find the ambusher who might well be still waiting for a better shot. Turning, he shouted to a frightened-looking employee, "Is there a back door to this place?"

"Straight down the aisle."

Longarm jumped up and ran down an aisle out onto a small loading dock. He sailed off the dock into the alley, and in a few moments he was back on the main street. Nothing moved on the street, and Longarm could see dozens of faces peering out at him through the storefront windows. A slovenly drunk emerged from a saloon, waved at Longarm, then shouted, "Fun is all over, Marshal! You can come out now and buy old Lester a bottle!"

To hell with old Lester, Longarm decided, moving cautiously out into the street and feeling his heart banging against his ribs.

From a second-story hotel room window just up the street, Longarm saw a curtain waving slightly in the breeze. Nothing unusual about that except that he could see the dim silhouette of a man. Still nothing unusual except that the next thing he saw was a rifle barrel sneaking out from under the curtain looking like a snake coming out of a hole.

Longarm's gun was still clenched in his fist. He fired without aiming, then fired again. He thought he heard a scream and was sure that the rifle barrel disappeared.

He sprinted toward the entrance to the hotel. If he was lucky, his ambusher was wounded and might prove to be a fountain of information concerning the Grand Canyon Gang.

If he was *unlucky,* his ambusher would be gone . . . or dead.

Chapter 13

The ambusher was propped up against the wall, head resting against the windowsill, dirty and faded yellow curtains flapping across his face. When Longarm burst into the hotel room, his first impression was that the ambusher was dead because there was blood all over the front of his shirt and his rifle lay just out of his reach. But that impression quickly changed when the ambusher dragged his six-gun out of his holster and tried to take aim and fire.

"Drop it!" Longarm ordered.

The man's face contorted into a grimace, and he kept trying to lift his pistol but it seemed to have become as heavy as a blacksmith's anvil. The man shook all over, and when he managed finally to pull the trigger, his errant bullet plowed into the floor not even near his intended target.

Longarm kicked the gun from the man's fist so hard that it went flying out the window into the street. He knelt beside the dying man. "Who are you?"

"Go to hell, Marshal Long."

"You know my name. At least tell me yours so I can notify your next of kin."

A terrible rattle sounded in the man's throat and he tried to work up a spit, but there was too much bright red froth so he barked a dying laugh. "My . . . my next of kin will be callin' on you soon enough."

The man was wearing a bowler, and when Longarm removed it, he saw a dirty mass of reddish-brown hair. He also judged that the ambusher was at least six feet tall. "You're a member of the Grand Canyon Gang."

It was a statement of fact, not a question, and the dying man made no effort at denial. "They'll do what . . . what I failed to do."

"Kill me?"

He nodded his head and coughed more blood. Longarm could see that he'd hit the ambusher in the right lung. "So they're going to come after me? Good. It'll save me a lot of time chasing them down."

The ambusher's eyes burned with intense hate. "I'll see you in hell, Marshal!" Then, he spat blood in Longarm's face.

Longarm reacted with a roar of indignation. His big hands shot out and grabbed the dying ambusher, then picked him up and hurled him through the open window. The dying killer's eyes widened with shock and then he disappeared. A moment later, Longarm heard a loud crash down on the boardwalk.

A quick examination of the room was made in case the dead man had some belongings that might give a clue as to his identity. But the hotel room was empty, and the only thing that gave evidence of what had just occurred were bloody smears under the windowsill and across the dirty yellow curtains.

Longarm went back down the hallway and stairs, then

stopped in front of the hotel clerk and said, "Do you know who the big man upstairs was?"

"Which big man?"

"The one with the reddish hair who tried to ambush me minutes ago."

"No sir." The clerk shook his head back and forth. "That room wasn't even rented. The man must have come up the back stairway, broke a lock, and sneaked inside."

Longarm didn't know whether to believe the clerk or not, so he went back out on the street. The dead man had struck the edge of the boardwalk, snapping his back. Twisted at an unnatural angle, his legs were sprawled across the walk and his shoulders and head were in the dirt beside a hitching rail. The two horses that had been tied to the rail were fighting to get away from the scent of fresh blood.

"Does anyone know this ambusher?" Longarm yelled, dragging the body into the middle of the street and sitting him upright, then turning him around in a full circle. "*Someone* must know him!"

People began to emerge from the stores and saloons. Death always attracted gawkers like carrion did buzzards. "Who knows this man?" Longarm challenged.

"I do," a firm and feminine voice declared.

Longarm turned and saw Victoria coming forward. "He's one of the big men I was telling you about."

"But you don't know his name?"

"I seem to remember they called him Jimmy. That's all I know," Victoria said.

Longarm wasn't satisfied. He dropped the body, put his hands on his hips, and surveyed the townspeople. "Who knows this man's complete name?"

Finally, a burly man stepped forward. "That's Jimmy Tyler. He's a mule skinner like me."

"And he has brothers?"

"Sure."

"Where can I find them?"

The mule skinner shrugged. "I see 'em around here and there, but they work for themselves. Reckon when they hear about this, they'll come to find you."

"That's fine with me," Longarm said loud enough for everyone to hear. "Does anyone else know a thing about this man or his brothers?"

"They have a ranch up near the rim of the canyon," a woman said.

"What's it called?"

"I don't know. I've heard that they run cattle, horses, and sheep."

"Thank you," Longarm told the woman. "Anyone happen to know the name of this man's ranch?"

A boy of about fifteen detached from the gawkers. He was tall, gangly, and wore no shoes, and there were big holes in the knees of his pants. "Jimmy Tyler and his brothers own a lotta land in this part of the country."

"What do you mean?"

The boy was extremely nervous and had to clear his throat. "They're a big family, and they don't live in just one spot. I hear they got a place down in Prescott, another north of Seligman, and maybe even more ranches and homesteads."

Longarm went over to the boy and shook his hand. "You're brave for telling me this." He looked around at the crowd and said loud enough for everyone to hear, "I wonder how many other people know what you've just told me but were too cowardly to step forward and speak up."

The boy gave Longarm a fleeting smile then backed into the crowd and disappeared.

Longarm reloaded his gun in the street while everyone watched in silence. Victoria came to stand by his side. "Can I buy you a drink, Marshal?"

"Sure," Longarm said, a moment before raising his voice loud enough so there was no mistaking his message. "Jimmy Tyler was one of the Grand Canyon Gang, and that means he was a thief, murderer, and rapist. I don't know if his family is also part of the gang, but I intend to find out. So if any of you are friends of the Tyler family, you'd better be watching for me, because I'll be coming around. And if you're in the gang, I'll find that out, too."

Longarm turned on his heel and walked with Victoria to her saloon. When they got inside, she ordered two double whiskies and a damp bar towel. She used the towel to wipe Longarm's face. "There's blood on your face. Did you get hurt?"

"Spat upon." Longarm took his whiskey and drank it down neat.

Victoria drained her own glass and signaled her bartender for refills. "Is that why you threw a dying man out a second-story window?"

"I expect so. Throwing Jimmy Tyler out the window wasn't something I'm particularly proud of. I lost my damned temper, that's all."

"I see."

Ollie appeared a few minutes later looking flushed and excited. Longarm also noticed that the giant had forgotten to button the fly on his pants, which were stained with wet spots. It was clear that Ollie and Big Annie had found a lot more in common than the fact that they were both big Swedes.

"I'm sorry I wasn't here sooner," Ollie apologized. "I was busy interviewing someone."

143

"I'm sure you were," Longarm said with amusement.

"What can I do now?"

"Go find a place to hide but where you can watch and see who collects the body."

"It's already been collected," Ollie told him.

"By who?"

"I don't know. When I came runnin' I saw three or four men dragging the body over to the undertaker."

"Go see if you can find out who they were and then stake out the undertaker's parlor," Longarm told his deputy. "If some big, redheaded men appear, I want you to come find me."

"And you'll be here?"

"Or upstairs in my room," Victoria said, pointing up to the second floor.

Ollie followed her finger and then looked at his boss. "I see."

"Just do what I told you," Longarm said. "Don't get into a fight, and don't let the men who came for the body see you watching. Understand?"

"Are they the gang?"

"Maybe part of it, at least."

"And you don't want me to try to arrest them?"

"No!"

Ollie backed up, shocked by Longarm's outburst. "I was just askin'. You don't have to yell at me, Custis."

"Sorry. But just do as I ask."

"Yes sir."

No sooner had Ollie left the Red Garter when in marched three men who stopped Longarm and Victoria as they were about to go upstairs.

"Marshal Long!"

Longarm turned to see Mayor Ed Wilson and two others of his kind, and they didn't look very happy. "We need to have a word with you right now, Marshal!"

"Speak your mind."

"Do you realize how many innocent people could have been shot and killed in our street a few minutes ago?"

"Yeah," Longarm said. "I do."

"Well then, what have you to say for yourself?"

Longarm frowned. "What do you mean?"

"How could you have been so stupid as to open fire in the middle of the street and risk innocent lives?" one of the other men demanded, clenching his fist and waving it in Longarm's face.

"Who are *you?*" Longarm demanded, batting the man's fist away.

He puffed up like a bullfrog and was just about as ugly. "My name is Mr. Horace J. Walker."

"Ah yes," Longarm said, "the man whose bank has been robbed twice and whose combination to the vault was mysteriously known by the gang . . . both times."

Walker's eyes widened behind his spectacles, and he assumed an expression of pure outrage. "Marshal, what are you insinuating?"

"Not a thing," Longarm told the man. "Except that I'm going to be coming around to ask you some hard questions in the next day or two. And, Mr. Walker, you'd better have some good answers."

Longarm's offensive had completely taken the wind out of Walker's sails. He shrank back behind the mayor and said no more.

"And there's another thing, Marshal Long," the mayor stammered, "I can't believe that you would be so . . . so barbaric . . . as to throw a dead man out a second-story window into the street. That was outrageous!"

"I knew the street was empty and that he wouldn't land

on anyone and hurt them. Besides, he wasn't completely dead."

"Worse yet!" the mayor screamed. "Who is your superior? I want you removed from this case immediately. And I intend to see if you can be charged with some crime."

Longarm laughed, and it wasn't a pretty sound. "Let me get this straight. A member of the Grand Canyon Gang tries to ambush a federal officer of the law who fires back and mortally wounds the ambusher. Then, the ambusher is tossed out the window, and you're telling me that *I* am at fault?"

When the mayor found himself at a loss for words, Longarm jabbed the third, stern-looking man in the chest. He wore a cheap black suit and a long black beard that needed to be washed and trimmed. "Who are you?"

"I am . . . am Reverend Benjamin McCallister," the minister said, seeming to rise up in his scuffed brown shoes. "And what you did to that man by throwing him out in the street was a *terrible* sin."

"He needed to die, Reverend."

"Only the Lord can choose the moment of a man's death."

"Not when he tries to kill me," Longarm argued. "Besides, Reverend, aren't you forgetting what this man has done to others?"

"It is always sinful to take a life in anger. And only an angry man would throw a dead man out of a window without regard to the horror it inflicted on Christian women, men, and little children."

"Alright," Longarm said, already growing weary of this conversation. "I shouldn't have done that. But I killed the man in self-defense. Jimmy Tyler took his last shot at me up in the hotel room, and I ended his life. I'll stand up to the law or the Lord, and they'll find me innocent."

"I think you are an immoral man," the reverend said, his voice rising. "And I think it would be best for Flagstaff if you left town on the next train."

Longarm sighed deeply. "I'm not leaving until I've finished my work here. That's the end of this discussion."

He slipped his arm around Victoria's waist and started up the stairs when the reverend called, "You have committed a mortal sin, and your soul shall be forever tainted with the blood of Jimmy Tyler."

"Better that than his soul forever be tainted with my blood," Longarm deadpanned as he led Victoria up the stairs to her room.

When they were relaxed and alone, stretched out on Victoria's bed, Longarm asked for a cigar and a brandy. They were given to him immediately, and the brandy was French and smooth as glass.

"Well, Custis," she said, "you've let it be known in no uncertain terms that you mean business."

"Will they really come after me?"

"I'm afraid so, and they won't fight fair."

"By that," Longarm said, "they'll come in numbers."

"Yes."

"Then I need to distance myself from you and this saloon," he told her as he climbed off the bed and reached for his coat.

"I didn't mean that you should leave."

"I know, but it's for the best. People will already be talking about us. Victoria, you're a good woman and you're also intelligent enough to know that whoever is with me is going to be in the eye of the storm."

She came and hugged him around the neck. "I don't want you to die."

"I don't want to die, either. Besides, I do have Ollie Swenson."

Victoria pulled back and shook her head. "The only thing he's good for is to stand behind when the bullets start coming your way."

"That's not true," Longarm told her. "Believe it or not, Ollie Swenson is a marksman with either a pistol or rifle. And he's brave and loyal, which are two qualities that should never be undervalued."

"I suppose not," Victoria said. "But I just wish there weren't so many who will now be wanting to kill you."

"I'm not going to be a sitting duck," he told her. "I've been up against long odds before and always managed to survive."

"But how could you . . ."

Longarm silenced her question with a kiss, then detached himself and reached for his hat. "I'm going to tell you something, Victoria, and I hope it makes you feel better."

"I'm listening."

"When you're up against long odds," Longarm said, "the thing that seems to work best is to take the attitude that you have the advantage, not your enemies."

"I don't understand."

"Take the offensive! Go after your enemies and try to take out their leaders when they are expecting you to have your tail between your legs and your knees knocking with fear."

"That's it?"

Longarm reached for the door. "That's it. I won't be sitting in the marshal's office waiting to be gunned down when I go to eat or step out for a breath of fresh air. No, ma'am! I'll be going after the ringleaders of this gang."

Victoria nodded and reached for the bottle. She poured a glass and raised it to Longarm in a toast, and Longarm saw that there were tears in her eyes.

Chapter 14

"Marshal Long?" Ollie said, peeking through the front door of the office.

Longarm looked up from his newspaper. "Yes?"

"I've been waiting for two days for Jimmy Tyler's kinfolks to come and claim the body for burial. Maybe they ain't coming."

"They'll be here," Longarm to his assistant. "Just keep your eye out for them and let me know the minute they arrive."

"But . . . but I'm getting' real tired of watchin' that funeral parlor," Ollie complained. "And the undertaker knows what I'm up to and keeps coming over and asking what he's supposed to do when the body begins to putrefy."

"Tell him to have patience."

"He says we need to get Tyler in the ground *today*, and he wants to know who is payin' for his services."

"Tell him Tyler's family will be arriving soon and that they'll pay."

"But what if they don't? We can't just . . ."

"Look!" Longarm exclaimed, jumping up from his chair and rushing over to the window as four grim-faced riders surrounding a buckboard came slowly up the street to stop in front of the funeral parlor. "Looks like we've got the company we've been waiting for."

Ollie's eyes grew wide with excitement. "I'll bet that's them, alright. What are we going to do, ambush 'em when they carry out Jimmy's body?"

"No," Longarm said. "We can't do that."

"Then what will we do against five armed men?"

Longarm thought about it a moment, then said, "I'll wait until they're ready to leave with Jimmy's body and then go out and have a talk with them. I want you to take a good firing position across the street. If they go for their guns, I'll be relying on your expert marksmanship."

"Why don't we try to get the drop on all five and then either shoot or arrest them before they decide to fight?"

"We don't yet have any evidence they are members of the gang."

"They look like they're related to Jimmy."

"I'm sure they are, but that doesn't mean anything in a court of law."

"We *got* to get the drop on them," Ollie said.

Longarm went over to the gun cabinet. "Would you like a rifle or a shotgun?"

"Both," the giant said.

Longarm gave his assistant a big double-barreled shotgun. "Use this for starters if there's gun trouble."

"I will," Ollie promised. "Given the odds against us, we can't wait for them to act first."

"Oh, but we'll have to," Longarm countered. "That's the way it works when you wear a badge, Ollie."

The big man grumbled as he loaded the shotgun and checked the rifle. "I'll be hiding across the street," he told

Longarm. "I'll open up on that bunch at the first sign that they're going to try and drop you, Custis."

"No," Longarm said. "If there's any shooting to be done, I'll do it first."

Ollie nodded with grudging acceptance, but the expression on his battered face told Longarm that he wasn't a bit happy.

Ten minutes passed before Longarm saw the Tyler men kick open the door to the funeral parlor and then carry out Jimmy's casket to be loaded on the buckboard. The mortician came running out, shouting something and clearly upset. One of the Tyler men acted as if he was coming over to pay the man, but instead punched the mortician in the face, dropping him to the ground. The mortician curled up in a ball and tried to protect himself from further punishment as the man began to kick him with both boots.

By then, Longarm was already out the door and moving swiftly across the street. He drew his gun and fired a warning shot over his head. "Enough!" he shouted.

All five of the Tyler clan turned as one and stared at Longarm.

"Are you the one who shot my son Jimmy?" the old man in the buckboard demanded, his face mottling with anger.

"I am," Longarm said, his gun swinging to point at the head of the clan. "Your son tried to ambush me from the second floor of a hotel."

"And then you tossed my boy's goddamn body out the window onto the boardwalk like you'd toss a piece of trash!"

"I sorta regret doing that," Longarm admitted. "But he was already as good as dead."

Longarm drew his six-gun and turned to the man who had punched and then kicked the undertaker. "You're under arrest for assault. Get over here."

The old patriarch in the buckboard had once been a big man, and he still had broad, impressive shoulders. His hair was mostly white, but there was still some washed-out red in it. He wore an old shirt and baggy pants, and a shotgun was resting across his lap. Now, he swore and shouted, "Benny, don't you go near that son of a bitch!"

Longarm cocked back the hammer of his gun and swung it on the old man. "If Benny doesn't do what I say, I'm killing you first."

"I ain't afraid of death. I've had plenty of years of livin' . . . but you ain't."

"And neither has Benny," Longarm said, his gun pointing at the old man's thick chest.

Tyler spat a stream of dark brown tobacco at Longarm, but it fell short. "We got us an interesting situation here," he said, almost as if he were trading a horse or cow. "Very interesting."

"It's your call," Longarm said.

Tyler nodded and turned to his sons and nephews. "Boys, if he kills me, you gun the marshal down like a dog, and when he's dead, you piss on his body. Piss on it right here in the street so everyone can see what the Tyler family does to those who cross 'em."

Longarm knew he was as close to dying as he'd ever been. The old patriarch wasn't bluffing, and he was filled with so much hate that he'd gladly die to take out a young and too brave lawman.

"Mr. Tyler," Longarm said. "Before we have a bloodbath in this street, you ought to know that I've got armed deputies hiding with rifles and shotguns ready to blow not only you, but Benny and all the rest into hell."

154

The old man swung his shaggy head all around, staring at the buildings and even up at the rooftops. He took his time, and when his inspection was finished, he smiled wickedly and said, "No you don't. You're bluffing, Marshal. And I reckon I'll call your bluff."

"If you do, it'll be the last one you ever call. And there won't be a Tyler standing when the lead stops flying."

"Pa," Benny said raising up both hands to his shoulders in a gesture of surrender, "maybe I ought to go to jail for a little while. I don't mind. I got my licks in, and we can settle things later, on *our terms*."

The old man chewed his tobacco faster, eyes still scanning the town for hidden riflemen. Finally, he spat again and said, "Benny, if you really want to do it that way, I'll go along."

Benny almost sagged, and the other three Tyler men looked almost as relieved.

"Marshal, where you from?" the old man asked, turning back to Longarm.

"Denver."

"Do you know how many men are in my family who will be after your head?"

Longarm shrugged to show he really didn't much give a damn. "Probably a dozen, give or take three or four."

Tyler's eyebrows shot up. "How'd you guess that?"

Longarm smiled. "Because that's how many members there are of the Grand Canyon Gang."

"Are you sayin' you think me and my boys and kinfolks are part of that bunch of thieves and murderers?"

"That's exactly what I'm thinking, Mr. Tyler."

"Ha! You're crazier than a damned bedbug! You got any evidence, Marshal nobody from Denver?"

"I can find some. It won't take long, given all the people you've killed, the women your boys have raped, and

155

your frequent thieving and robbing of banks."

Tyler's face hardened. "You're a fool, Marshal. You ride into this country not knowing anything and then you start making charges you can't back up. Is that how it works over in Colorado?"

"It works the same way everywhere, Mr. Tyler. I just need to find some witnesses."

"You won't find a single damned one. Most Arizona folks are a whole lot smarter than you are. They know they need to keep their mouths shut and not go accusing me or my kin of wrongdoing. That wouldn't be healthy."

Longarm didn't take his eye off the old man. "Benny, put your hands over your head and get over here."

Benny grinned. "Sure is gonna be fun pissing on your bullet-riddled body."

"I wouldn't count on doing it," Longarm told the cocky kid who looked to be about twenty years old.

"You really are dumb," Benny said with a mocking laugh. "Why . . ."

Longarm backhanded the kid across the mouth so hard Benny staggered and dropped to one knee. Tyler started to lift his shotgun, and Longarm shouted, "Don't do it!"

The old man froze, his eyes filled with hatred. "You killed Jimmy, and now you've just laid a hand on my son Benny. Marshal, I can't wait to bring you down. I'll have you begging for mercy."

"Big talk for a man who says he's not afraid to die but won't lift a hand when it counts."

"Pa, no!" one of the men cried.

But the old man was too filled with rage, arrogance, and hatred to listen. He raised the shotgun, and just as he was about to fire, Longarm pulled the trigger of his Colt revolver. His bullet struck Tyler in the throat, tearing it open. The old man let out a strangled cry, grabbed his

156

neck, and toppled off the wagon, kicking and twitching in the dirt. A moment later, Benny let out a scream of rage and his hand went for his gun; that's when Ollie Swenson opened up with the double-barreled shotgun.

Benny was lifted completely off the ground and hurled into a hitching rail. Longarm jumped behind a horse water trough, but when he saw the last three Tyler men dive behind the buckboard then throw up their hands in surrender, he shouted, "Ollie, no more!"

The giant emerged from the shadows with the shotgun looking like just a child's toy in his massive fists. He marched up to the three Tyler men crouched behind the buckboard and said, "You boys chicken? Not ready to die?"

Longarm hurried over to Ollie. "Don't shoot them."

"Why not?" Ollie said. "Better now than later."

"It would be murder," Longarm explained. "Ollie, put down the shotgun."

"We ain't done a thing!" one of them swore, tears streaming down his cheeks. "We just came to pick up Jimmy's body, and now you've gone and killed Benny and Pa, too!"

"Your father was filled with poison, and it made him do something very stupid," Longarm said. "Not only did it get him killed, but it also got Benny killed. Now, the question is, are you three ready to go to the graveyard with them?"

The three Tyler men were all crying, but it wasn't because they were scared as much as it was because of their grief, helplessness, and hatred. Longarm knew he had no cause to arrest them, for they had taken no action against the law. And yet, he also realized that it would be a terrible mistake to let them go get other members of their family as well as their friends and come storming back to Flagstaff seeking bloody revenge.

"You three are under arrest," he said, making a decision.

"On what charges?"

"Obstructing justice."

"We ain't done nothin' yet! You and that big bastard have done all the killing so far."

"Ollie," Longarm said, "disarm them and take them to jail."

"What about Jimmy, Benny, and my pa!"

"You're right," Longarm said. "What's your name?"

"Zane Tyler."

"Well, Zane," Longarm said, "I'm going to let you take these bodies back to your ranch or wherever it is that you bury your kinfolks. Plant them and tell the rest of your gang that I'm going to be coming after them and I'll get my evidence—enough evidence not only to hang these two I'm taking to jail, but enough to see that you and the others hang after being sentenced by a judge."

Zane didn't say a word.

"Did you hear me?" Longarm repeated, stepping in close to the man so they were nose to nose.

"I heard you, Marshal. I heard you well. And I'll be seeing you real soon."

Longarm disarmed Zane and told him to get busy loading the dead and then to get them the hell out of Flagstaff.

He watched Ollie lead their two prisoners to the jail, and he waited until Zane had Jimmy, Benny, and their father loaded in the buckboard and then left town.

Mayor Ed Wilson hurried out to join Longarm. "Now you've really done it, Marshal! Now we're going to have a war right here in the middle of my town! And innocent people are probably going to die all because of your stupidity."

Longarm whirled on the mayor, grabbed him by the front of his coat, and shoved him backward a dozen feet before dumping him into the horse water trough. For good measure, he held Wilson's head underwater for a full minute, and when he let the man up for air, the mayor was pale and shaking.

"You've just been baptized in the waters of *truth*," Longarm hissed. "Do you see the light, or are you still blind?"

"I . . . I'll have you . . ."

Longarm shoved the mayor's head under again and held it even longer. He stared at the man's eyes bulging in terror, and this time when he lifted Mayor Wilson up by his hair and asked if he had seen the truth, Wilson screamed, "Yes!"

"Glad to hear it," Longarm growled as he headed for his office.

Chapter 15

Longarm lit a cheroot and paced slowly back and forth in the marshal's office, his mind wrestling with his next course of action against the Grand Canyon Gang. He looked out the window and saw that the sun was setting in the west. Behind him, Ollie Swenson sat squeezed into an office chair, and their two prisoners sat huddled together in the town jail.

"What are we going to do now?" Ollie finally asked. "If we sit here and wait for the gang to come, we'll be sitting ducks."

"We're not waiting."

Ollie stood up. "Are we going after them?"

Longarm saw that the Tyler brothers had stopped talking and were all ears, so he turned to Ollie and motioned for them to step outside so they could speak in private. Shutting the door behind him and escorting Ollie aside, Longarm said, "We're getting out of here tonight."

"We are?"

"Yeah."

"What about those two prisoners?"

"We'll learn what we can from them and then take them with us when we go to arrest the gang."

But Ollie shook his head. "You really think those two Tyler boys will cooperate? They seem mighty tough, and they'll know their own hash is cooked if word gets back to their kinfolks that they helped us."

"I know that." Longarm frowned. "We'll have to trick them somehow."

"I don't follow you, Custis."

"Let's make them think that we're against each other as well as being weak and afraid."

"I am kind of afraid," Ollie admitted. "When the Tyler bunch finds out that three of their own are dead, there will be hell to pay. They'll come riding in here with blood in their eyes and their guns smokin'."

"Not if we get to them before they can all gather and organize an attack," Longarm said. "And to do that, we need to know where they are and how many to expect. The only way we can find out that information is for those two boys inside to tell us."

"I'm listening. Keep talking."

"We'll get whiskey bottles filled with tea and act drunk in our office. Then, we'll fake a fight and I'll storm out, threatening to come back and kill all three of you."

"What?"

"It'll just be a threat," Longarm said. "But when I leave, you act as if I really meant what I said and ask the Tylers if they want to make a deal."

"What deal?"

"You'll let them out of jail if they take you to the rest of the bunch so I can't kill you."

"And you think they'll believe that?"

"We have to *make* them believe it," Longarm said. "We

162

have to go in there with whiskey bottles in our fists and malice toward each other in our minds."

"What's malice?"

"Hatred," Longarm said. "We'll argue and then fight. You'll win, but I'll leave, vowing to soon return and kill you three. That way, the Tyler boys will be under a lot of pressure to help you if you help them in return."

"It might work."

"It will work," Longarm promised. "But you have to get the names of all the members of the Grand Canyon Gang. Don't write them down, because that would tip our hand. But remember where we can find them."

"I'll try," Ollie said, looking worried. "Are we going to really hit each other?"

"Yes, but pull your punches and I'll do the same."

"I don't want to hurt you, Custis. Even pulling punches I could hurt you."

"Just make it look good. When the Tyler boys tell you as much as you can learn, let them out of the jail with their promise that you can ride with them. I'll follow. When we get close to having a showdown, we've just got to get the job done or else we're finished."

Ollie rubbed his jaw. "You sure there ain't a better way to do this? Sounds like a lot could go wrong. And I don't want to fight you, Custis, even if it is only a trick."

"Look," Longarm explained. "We have to get them to talk and to talk fast. And once they do and you turn them free, you'll look like their friend. They'll lead you to where the rest of them are hiding. I'll follow, and we'll take it from there."

"But what if some of 'em *don't* come? Like the ones in Prescott and other places?"

"Let's just take on what we can get right now, and if we pull it off, we'll go after the rest later."

"Alright," Ollie said, looking highly skeptical.

"Let's go over to the Red Garter Saloon and get some tea-filled whiskey bottles from Victoria and then hurry back here and put on a show for the Tylers."

"I'd like to tell Big Annie our plan first and . . ."

"No," Longarm said. "Let's keep it between ourselves and Victoria."

Ollie didn't look too happy about that, but he nodded his head in reluctant agreement.

Their plan went better than Longarm could have imagined. With Victoria's help and a little coaching for Ollie, they had returned to the marshal's office looking, smelling, and acting drunk, mad, and at each other's throats. Ollie had accused Longarm of being a fool and getting them into a deadly fix.

Acting enraged and frightened, Ollie hollered, "When all the Tyler men come back, they'll kill us and there's no one who will even lift a finger in this town to help save our asses!"

To which Longarm, weaving and waving his bottle of tea had shouted, "Are you a federal marshal or a damned coward?"

The argument was convincing, but the fight itself did not go off quite as well as expected. Longarm started the fray when he popped Ollie with a straight right to the nose, and damned if it didn't break and send blood cascading down the giant's lower face. Ollie, upset by the damage to his nose, hit Longarm a crunching blow to the side of the jaw that slammed him up against the bars and knocked him dizzy. When Ollie, his mouth and chin a mask of red gore, attacked again, Longarm kicked the giant between the legs hard enough to make him double up in agony. Longarm hammered his deputy in his ear and knocked him to the floor.

"Get up!" Longarm shouted. "Get up and fight, you coward!"

Ollie seemed to have forgotten that this was only a *pretend* fight, one designed to trick their prisoners. Nose broken and balls busted, he tackled Longarm, lifting him completely off the ground and carrying him through the doorway and out into the street.

"Stop it!" Longarm shouted as Ollie raised a fist to club him into unconsciousness. "We've done the job."

"Custis, you broke my nose!"

"I'm sorry."

"And kicked me in the balls!"

"I got carried away, but you cracked my skull against the jail bars and I'm still seeing double."

Longarm tore loose of the man, and when he saw that a crowd was already gathering, he shouted, "Ollie, you're fired! I'm gonna come back and kill all three of you bastards!"

Then Longarm staggered away, hoping that Ollie would rush back into the office and convince the Tyler boys that all their lives were about to end.

Ten minutes later, Longarm and Victoria watched from her upstairs room while Ollie and the two Tyler brothers exited the marshal's office. Darkness had fallen over the town, but, in the smoky glow of lamplights, it was easy to pick out the huge Ollie as he hurried down the street toward a stable.

"I'd better get a horse and get moving," Longarm said.

"I have some help for you," Victoria told him.

"What help?"

"Some of my best customers and friends are the Navajo. I let those who behave themselves drink in here when no other saloon owner will have them."

165

"Yeah," Longarm said, "I've seen them downstairs. They stick to themselves and stay quiet."

"I cut off their liquor if they get loud or drunk. Some of them just come in and drink sarsaparilla, and they love to hear the piano music. I like those Indians and make sure no one gives them any problems."

"But what . . ."

"I told them about what you're doing, and they want to help."

"Indians?"

"Navajo. Dine. They've lost a lot of sheep, and several of their women have been raped or insulted. There are five of them, and they want to bring the Grand Canyon Gang to justice."

"Victoria," Longarm mused, "I appreciate the thought, but . . ."

"Don't be a fool," Victoria interrupted. "These Navajo are the best trackers you'll ever find outside of the Apache. They're good shots, and I promise they won't betray you. You couldn't have a better posse riding at your side tonight than these reservation Navajo."

"Alright," Longarm said, knowing he'd have to have some help or the odds against himself and Ollie were terrible. "Let's go down and I'll meet them. Do they speak English?"

"Some do, some don't. But the ones who do will translate for the ones who don't. And they hate Tyler men to the bone."

"Alright," Longarm said, staring to feel that he'd finally been given a winning hand. "But they have to agree to follow my orders. I won't have them open fire and massacre the Tylers."

"I've already explained that to Niache. He's their leader, and he agrees that you will be in charge."

Longarm shook his head and clamped his hands over his ears.

"Something wrong?" Victoria asked, looking worried.

"My ears are still ringing from the punch I took from Ollie and from my head being slammed up against the cell bars."

"He shouldn't have done that! Didn't you tell that big ox to pull his punches?"

"Yeah. But after I broke his nose and kicked him in the balls, Ollie sorta forgot the rules."

Victoria's eyes widened. "If you did that, you deserve what you got, Custis."

"I expect so," Longarm ruefully admitted. "Let's go meet Niache and his Navajo trackers and fighters."

The Navajo were stocky, quiet men, and when they saw Longarm and Victoria coming to their table, they swept their dominos into a leather bag and stood up as a sign of respect and greeting.

"Niache," Victoria said, "this is United States Marshal Custis Long. He's got a deputy with the two Tyler boys, and they're heading for reinforcements. I told Marshal Long that you and your men would not be afraid to ride and fight with him."

Niache was about Longarm's age and stood about five foot ten inches. His hair was long, and there were silver threads among the black. He had piercing black eyes and a calm demeanor. He stuck out his hand, and when Longarm took it in his own, it felt as hard and rough as a chunk of volcanic lava.

Longarm said, "My deputy's life is in danger. We must follow and find the Tyler bunch, and there will probably be a bad fight. I need men who will fight hard and not run even if some of us are killed."

Niache nodded gravely and then translated to those of his men who did not understand English. Every one of the Navajo then extended their hand to Longarm in a clear demonstration that they would, indeed, fight to the death.

Victoria slipped her arm around Longarm's waist. "This is my man," she told the Navajo. "I want him back. But I also want the big one . . . the giant to come back alive."

Niache said, "My people have lost many sheep, and our women and children have been insulted and hurt. It is time that we kill these Tyler men so they will no more hurt the Dine."

"I agree," Longarm said. "And now we must ride before we lose their trail."

Quickly, Niache translated and then the Navajo were hurrying to leave the Red Garter. White men standing at the long bar or sitting at the tables watched with questioning eyes, but neither Victoria or Longarm offered them any explanation.

"Kiss me good-bye and promise that you'll come back in one piece," Victoria pleaded as they stood outside for a moment.

"I'll come back in one piece," Longarm promised, taking her into his arms and kissing her sweet lips. "And thanks for the reinforcements."

"Niache will not betray you, Custis. And he and his men will fight well."

"I know that without a shadow of a doubt."

The Navajo were mounted, and Niache handed Longarm the reins to a saddled Indian pony. It was a paint horse, small but strong and feisty. Longarm was grateful that the Indians had even adjusted the stirrups to accommodate his long legs.

And then, with a wave of good-bye to Victoria, they went galloping out of town, heading north toward the Tyler family stronghold, which was also that of the Grand Canyon Gang.

Longarm was sure they would be there before daybreak. And he was just as certain that, as sure as the sunrise would fire the magnificence of the Grand Canyon, many tough white men and Navajo would soon die.

Chapter 16

Darkness had fallen completely, and there was only a thin
sliver of moon up in the night sky when Longarm and the
Navajo picked up the trail of Ollie and the Tyler men.
The trail they followed started north and climbed through
heavy Ponderosa Pine forests for six or seven miles, pass-
ing on the western slopes of the San Francisco Peaks. The
tallest of these peaks was Mt. Humphreys, standing
12,643 feet. Humphreys Peak was snowcapped, and the
air was cool and crisp as they rode single file, Niache in
the lead, followed by two of his best trackers with Longarm riding in the middle.

The Navajo's horses were short, tough beasts with un-
shod hooves and no fat on their ribs. Longarm's pony was
a pinto, as were many of the others, and he didn't have
to use the reins because the pony followed the others,
walking fast and making almost no sound. They passed
through the Ponderosas and entered a high plateau thick
with the squatty silhouettes of piñon and juniper. The
ground was littered with volcanic cinder, and the trail they

followed was like a pale string stretched straight across the rocky, dark earth floor.

Longarm saw cattle standing in the pale moonlight and plenty of deer and elk. He heard coyotes calling in the distance and thought he heard the tinkle of a goat's bell and imagined there might be a flock of sheep in the hills nearby.

After hours of riding, they came to a stream and rested their horses. Longarm sought out Niache and asked him how much farther they could expect yet to travel. The Navajo warrior pointed to the northwest and said that they would be at the Tyler ranch an hour before daybreak.

There wasn't much else to do but let the Indians lead the way, and as the night passed, Longarm couldn't help but wonder what Ollie must be thinking, for, if anything, his predicament was far more precarious than Longarm's. Ollie would feel like Jonah being swallowed alive by the whale. He would be immediately suspect, and the Tylers, having lost their leader and two more of their kin, one of them killed by Ollie's shotgun, would not be in a trusting or forgiving mood.

Longarm wondered if Ollie stood any chance of surviving, and the more thought he gave the question, the more he decided that he would have to strike the gang quickly and with a great deal of firepower if his deputy was to survive.

Longarm judged it was around four in the morning when the Navajo dismounted, checking their pistols and rifles. After making sure his own weapons were in order, Longarm paused and listened carefully. He could hear the low of cattle and the bawling of what he presumed were even more stolen Navajo sheep. Niache indicated that they were almost at the Tyler ranch, which was nestled in a valley just beyond a low rise just up ahead. After tying their horses to junipers, they climbed the rise to gaze down on the ranch.

"It's about what I'd expect," Longarm told Niache. "Ranch house. Corrals and outbuildings. How many of them do you think are left?"

Niache shrugged, because it was too dark to even count horses.

"We've about an hour to daybreak," Longarm said. "There's just one light on in the house. Niache, I'm going in, and I want you and your men to follow but to fan out and stay back about fifty yards from the house. I'm going to try and get to my deputy, then see what happens."

The Navajo listened carefully. "Before the sun rises off the land, they will all be dead."

Longarm didn't know what to say in response. He was hoping for surrender, but the Navajo knew as well as he did that wasn't realistic. This was the home of the Grand Canyon Gang, and these men were not going to surrender just so they could face a judge, jury, and then a hangman.

"All right," he said, "let's move. And when the shooting starts, let's make sure we don't kill each other in the darkness by mistake."

Niache relayed that message to his companions, and one of them actually giggled. That told Longarm he was working with a very cool party of fighters.

Longarm moved down from the rise, making as much noise by himself as did all of the Navajo. The ground was very rough, covered with rocks, brush, and even small cactus until they reached the perimeter of the yard where they came upon a corral of horses. Niache slipped through the pole corral and moments later returned from the darkness and whispered, "Three horses, wet and hot."

Longarm understood what the man was saying, and he motioned for the Navajo to spread out and wait while he went to the house and determined if he could locate and remove Ollie before the shooting started.

He was doing just fine and had crossed the yard and was about to climb up on a rickety old front porch when a large dog jumped out from under the porch floor and began to snarl and bark.

"Shhh!" Longarm whispered frantically.

It was too late. Lights went on in the house, and Longarm heard shouting and then one man yelled, "Dog, shut up or I'm gonna come out there and shoot ya!"

Longarm froze, and when he began to whisper endearments to the big cur, it quit growling and climbed back under the porch.

He waited for several minutes and then tiptoed to the front door. It creaked when he opened it and slipped quietly inside. Trying to adjust his eyes to an even deeper darkness, Longarm walked right into a man.

His rifle was in his left hand and his revolver in his right. Longarm lashed out hard with the pistol and heard it crack solidly on flesh and bone. A weight dropped, and it sounded like a ton of beef hitting a slaughterhouse floor. Longarm knelt beside the dark bulk and knew from the moment he smelled and touched the unconscious man that he had knocked Ollie Swenson out cold.

He swore under his breath and froze in a crouched position fully expecting someone else to be roused by the sound of Ollie's body striking the planks. But no one roused, and after a few moments, Longarm holstered his gun, leaned his rifle against a wall, and grabbed Ollie by the shirt. He slowly dragged the giant out the front door, and onto the porch. Once again, the big dog emerged, growling and barking. Once again, someone from inside yelled, "Shut the hell up!"

Longarm dragged Ollie off the porch and across the

yard. The man was such a ponderous dead weight that Longarm's breath was coming in short gasps by the time he got the Swede out beyond the corral and found a Navajo.

"Watch over him," he whispered, not knowing if this particular Indian understood the command.

Longarm headed back across the yard. Horses stomped restlessly in the corrals, all of them probably stolen. Two roosters began a crowing competition, and an owl sailed over the pines and into the rafters of the decrepit barn with a prairie dog firmly in its claws. Off to the east, the sky was turning from black to gray to a salmon color that would have been spectacular if there had been clouds on the horizon. And when the light grew just a little bit stronger, Longarm's jaw dropped when he realized that he was standing right on the south rim of the Grand Canyon. Vast, empty, filled with shadows, and bursting with emerging colors, it almost compelled him to stare. However, standing in the middle of the Tyler Ranch yard at sunrise would have been the height of foolishness.

So Longarm went back to the big, ramshackle house and again eased up on the porch. And for the third time, the dog came out growling, snarling, and barking.

"That's it!" someone inside bellowed, "I'm going to shoot you in the damned head this time!"

Longarm had the front door half open when one of the Tyler men came barreling his way through the house with curses on his lips and a gun in his fist.

"Hold it," Longarm said, hoping the man might be reasonable and drop his gun. But either the man didn't see the weapon in Longarm's fist, or else he was so startled that he shot in surprise. It didn't matter. Longarm felt the bullet tug at his gun belt and then he returned fire. The man crashed into a table, and dishes shattered on the floor.

After that, everyone in the place was coming out of their beds with their guns drawn. Longarm decided he was in a damned poor defensive position. He retreated to the porch, then turned and sprinted for the nearest cover, which happened to be the Tyler outhouse.

He had not quite reached the back of the shitter when a hail of bullets erupted from the front porch, but by then Longarm was diving for cover.

The Tyler men must have thought he was an idiot who had come alone, for they rushed out of the house, guns blazing. The Navajo waited until they were almost to the outhouse and out of bullets. Then, the Indians opened fire with their rifles, and when the smoke cleared and the screams fell silent on quivering lips, eight Tyler men were dead, some riddled by as many as ten Navajo bullets.

The sun came off the horizon, the Grand Canyon blazed with color, and Ollie Swenson was still unconscious.

"I hit him way too hard," Longarm fretted. "In the darkness of the house, I thought he was one of them."

"His head is cracked a little," Niache said, standing over the unconscious giant. "Blood comes from his ears."

"I might have killed him or . . . even worse . . . turned his brains to mush," Longarm said, disconsolate at the thought. "We've got to get him back to a doctor."

"Navajo medicine man better."

Longarm studied the Indian for a moment and then said, "Are you a medicine man?"

"No," Niache said, pointing to one of his men. "Ha-sha-mi is a good medicine man."

"Then ask him what he can do for my poor deputy."

Niache went to the medicine man who had been watching Ollie with great interest. Now, Ha-sha-mi came forward, knelt beside the giant, then gently rolled his head from side to side examining the ears. He felt Ollie's skull, said something to Niache, and hurried off into the brush.

"Where's he going?" Longarm asked.

"To get medicine roots. He'll be back soon."

Longarm sure hoped so. Ollie's breathing was shallow, and his color was poor although the early morning light might have had something to do with his gray complexion. And his face, with a freshly broken nose all purple and swollen, made him look even worse.

"Deputy Marshal Swenson," Longarm said to the man from Santa Fe, "if you survive this I'll owe you about anything you ask. I haven't treated you well in the last twenty-four hours, and I'm downright sorry about that."

Longarm went to take care of the business of death. He knew the Navajo would not wish to handle the bodies of the dead Tyler men, and he suspected that they would not want to be seen with them, either. Because, although the Tyler men were outlaws and killers, people in the West still couldn't stomach the idea of an Indian killing a white man, even when he might have overwhelming justification.

So one by one, Longarm dragged the bodies over to the old barn. He laid them out and thought he might load them in wagons and return them to Flagstaff. Then he decided that there was really no point in going to so much effort for such rotten sons of bitches.

So he shooed the owl out of the rafters and put a match to the barn. Once he was satisfied it would burn to the ground, Longarm went over to the ranch house while the Navajo stared at the hungry flames. In thirty minutes, Longarm dragged almost twenty thousand dollars and several satchels of jewelry out of the ranch house and placed them in the buckboard.

"It's done here," he told the Navajo. "Take all the sheep that are yours and whatever other livestock are either yours or have no brands. Take them back to your reservation with my thanks."

"What about your big friend?"

"It'll take at least three of us to lift him into the back of the buckboard. Has your medicine man been able to help him?"

Niache shrugged. "Too soon to know. Maybe help. Maybe not. Medicine good but takes longer."

"I understand."

They hitched up the buckboard with two horses and Longarm waved good-bye to the Navajo after wishing them well and giving them each a hundred dollars. Maybe that was illegal or improper because the money was stolen, but he didn't care. Without Niache and his friends, Longarm would have been nothing but riddled meat lying in a cloud of flies beside a shitter.

When the Navajo were gone, he torched the Tyler Ranch house and didn't even look back to watch it burn.

Did this finish his time in Arizona? And what about his deputy? If Ollie survived, Longarm decided that he would fire the man but let him keep his badge. Ollie just wasn't cut out for being a federal officer of the law. It was too hard on him physically.

Chapter 17

Even before Longarm got Ollie back to Flagstaff, his deputy was already beginning to come around and ask questions from the floor of the buckboard—not good or sensible questions, but questions nonetheless.

"Do you mean to say that I was knocked out cold during the whole danged gunfight with the Grand Canyon Gang?"

"I'm afraid so."

"And your posse was a band of Navajo Indians?"

"Yep. And I couldn't have asked for better."

"Damnation!" Ollie wailed. "I wanted to get in on that fight."

Longarm shrugged. "There will always be other fights."

"I sure hope so. I guess I didn't do much good in this one. What happened to me?"

Longarm had been dreading that question, but there was no getting around it. So he stopped the buckboard and turned around to look down at poor Ollie. "To be honest, I mistakenly pistol-whipped you in that dark Tyler house."

"*You* pistol-whipped me?"

"Yeah," Longarm confessed. "And I'm sorry."

Ollie didn't get off the bed of the wagon, but he shook his head slowly back and forth. "Damn, Custis, first you break my nose, then you almost kick my balls off, and finally you crack my skull with your pistol. Are you fixin' to shoot me any minute now?"

Longarm chuckled. "Nope. But you promised you'd tell me where I can find Emerald Alexander. After I throw Flagstaff's crooked banker in jail, Miss Alexander is the last piece of business I need to take care of in Arizona."

"So we're finished with the Grand Canyon Gang?" Ollie asked, sounding disappointed.

"I expect there are a few left who will be running from the law, but the power of the gang is broken. I've recovered a lot of the stolen goods, and the Navajo took back their livestock. Once Flagstaff gets a good and honest marshal, I am sure this part of the country will return to normal."

"Yeah, I guess it will. Say, Custis?"

"What?"

"Can I go down to Prescott with you to arrest Mrs. Patterson?"

"Who is she?"

"That's the one you call Miss Emerald Alexander."

"Thanks for that bit of information. But, Ollie, you're needed more in Flagstaff than in Prescott. Any interest in being Flagstaff's new town marshal?"

"You mean giving up on being a federal lawman?"

"In Flagstaff, you'd be the number one honcho. You'd be making far more money than me."

"I would?"

"Sure! And I'll even let you arrest that crooked banker. That's sure to get you the job and lots of respect."

180

Ollie closed his eyes. "I don't know," he said. "I'd have to give up my federal officer's badge."

"Make the town give you a badge even finer than I wear."

"I could do that?"

"I'll even stay in town a few days to help you negotiate the things you'll need, including your own deputy."

Ollie beamed. "You've been rough on me, but I know you didn't mean to do such damage. I'd like to be the marshal of Flagstaff. Big Annie would be proud of me. Maybe . . . maybe we'd even get married."

"I think that would be a fine idea," Longarm told his friend.

Ten days later, with Marshal Ollie Swenson in charge of Flagstaff, the banker in jail for confessing to robbery, and the mayor and entire town council fired and replaced by honest citizens, Longarm stepped off a train in Prescott. Originally an important U.S. Army post, it was now a bustling city whose leading citizens had raised enough cash to run a railroad line up to Ash Fork so they would be connected to the Santa Fe Railroad. Everything about Prescott looked prosperous, and Longarm was feeling quite pleased with Arizona when he surveyed the plaza and headed off to confront the deceitful Miss Emerald Alexander and retrieve his stolen travel money.

Ollie had said that Emerald was a rich widow, wife of a lumber mill tycoon, and that she lived in a mansion just two blocks east of the plaza. Longarm had no trouble finding the house, and when he knocked on Emerald's door, she almost fell over with shock.

"Hello, Mrs. Patterson. That is your real name, isn't it?"

She recovered quickly. "Why Marshal Custis Long! What a pleasant surprise."

"Glad to hear you say that. May I come inside?"

"Of course!"

Longarm removed his hat and entered the grand hallway decorated with fine French paintings, Greek statues, and an oriental carpet. "I'm glad to see you're doing so well."

"Thank you," she told him as she led the way into a comfortable parlor and indicated for him to take a seat. "Can I offer you refreshments?"

"Brandy sounds good."

"Certainly," she said.

Longarm looked around at all the books and expensive furniture. "What I want to know, Emerald, is . . . if you were rich . . . why did you steal from me on the train?"

She smiled. "Old habits die hard. I've been trying to reform, but after fleecing men for many years, it's never easy. But now I'm a lady."

"Are you really?" he asked.

Emerald giggled and shrugged her lovely shoulders. "In truth, I've never been a lady. I just happened to get lucky a few years ago and marry a rich man who adored me, then died and left me a rich widow."

"I'm still not convinced of why you stole my travel money."

Emerald's lovely smile faded, and she looked at him with a serious expression. "Custis, even if I told you the truth, I doubt you'd believe me."

"Try me," Longarm urged.

"Alright. When we were on the train, I knew your pride would be so injured when I lifted your money that you wouldn't rest until you found me."

"Come on!"

"I mean it. And I *wanted* you to find me."

He was genuinely confused. "But why?"

"Because I wanted to have you come to this mansion so I could take you to my bed."

Longarm's jaw dropped.

"I never liked making love on a train," she continued. "But upstairs, in my big feather bed, I am a . . . well, this sounds awful . . . I'm a tiger. A raging Amazon woman."

He gulped down some brandy. "Woman, are you willing to prove it right now?"

She began to undress right in the parlor.

"I'll still want my stolen money back," he said, his voice thickening with desire.

"You'll get your money and a *whole* lot more," Emerald promised as she led him out of the parlor, up the stairs, and into her bedroom.

Watch for

LONGARM AND THE GREAT MILK TRAIN ROBBERY

304th novel in the exciting LONGARM series
from Jove

Coming in March!

Explore the exciting Old West with one of the men who made it wild!

J. R. ROBERTS
THE
GUNSMITH